His

Sanctuary

By

Ronna M. Bacon

Psalms 5:11 But let all who take refuge in you be glad; let them ever sing for joy. Spread your protection over them, that those who love your name may rejoice in you.

Table of Contents

Chapter 1

Throwing his bag back onto the seat of his beat-up truck, Nigel Wells brushed an arm across his forehead, his eyes watching the activity around him, not quite sure he was ready to stay in this town. Something was definitely different here, and he could feel evil around him. No one looked directly at him, shooting off side glances as they scurried past him. He sighed, looking down at his worn and dusty clothes. He hadn't had a chance to change, not since he had stopped by the side of the road to check out the back tire and had to jump for the ditch to avoid being run down. Not the welcome he would have expected, not in a town named Sanctuary.

He looked around again. No, this was not the town he had been heading for. Somehow, he had taken a wrong turn. He'd grab something to eat and then head out again.

He wiped at his brow again, feeling the sweat gathering there. He hadn't been feeling great yesterday when he set out, on the open road, no destination in sight. Just a well deserved vacation and nobody to demand his time. He staggered for a moment, his hand going out to brace himself on the truck.

Hearing running steps behind him, he tried to turn, but instead was slammed into the truck, and then to the well worn dirt of the road, track, whatever you wanted to call it, he wasn't quite sure. The breath knocked out of him, he struggled to escape the hands holding him down before he was dragged to his feet and propelled into a nearby business.

He was shoved down into a chair, his arms clamped down on the chair arms by the strong hands from the men who surrounded him. He could hear shouted questions, the noise becoming a dull roar in his ears as he shook his head to clear it, knowing he was losing that battle.

He couldn't get his tongue to form a response, the fever that struck him taking that ability away from him. He slumped even more, not feeling the hands moving away from him, not hearing the murmurs around him. He didn't feel the soft hand of his cheek, or the young woman's barked commands that were ignored.

He finally roused at a question close to him, asking if he had a wife or a girlfriend, his head shaking in the negative, not quite sure what was being asked or why. He responded to questions being asked before he was helped to his feet once more and with someone's arm around his waist, led from the building and gently shoved into the passenger's side of his vehicle. He slumped, eyes closed, barely conscious as the truck shifted with the weight of another person sliding behind the wheel and then he felt the truck moving away.

Watching from a distance as the stranger was shoved into the town hall, Havan O'Leary had considered her position in town as she finally walked forward and into the room. She could hear the questions being fired rapidly at the man and saw his lack of response, a frown on her face as she studied him and realized just how close to passing out he was. She frowned once more and then moved forward, forcing the men holding him away until she could place a hand on his face and then on his shoulder, spinning to face the leader of the men, the town's mayor, a man she hated with a passion and had no idea why.

The mayor looked her up and down and snorted with derision, knowing she was there only to prevent him from going ahead with his plans. He had been waiting for a stranger to come to town, and now here he was.

Havan had stooped, asking the man quietly some questions, before she stood, her eyes steady on the man in front of her, showing no fear.

"You're not marrying him to your daughter, Brown. That's a given."

The mayor snorted. "I am. She's on her way right now."

"Sorry, mayor. You're not. He just agreed to marry me. Once word is given, you can't make anyone change their mind." She stood, almost toe to toe to him, feeling the venom and hatred spewing from him as he realized he had been outsmarted once more, that the law he had brought in to marry off his daughters had been used against him once more.

Havan stood beside the stranger as she heard the words that were uttered by the town minister, a man so scared by the mayor he could hardly speak. She watched as wedding bands were handed to the man and then to herself, fitting hers on her own finger and then the band onto his. She finally pulled him to his feet and out of the building, relieved at saving him, but knowing that their trouble had just begun. The mayor would see to that.

Lord, what did I just go and do? I couldn't stand by, not and see his life ruined by the mayor. That's a given. Please, dear Lord, guide for now. I'm in over my head and have no idea where this is going. She paused at an intersection, almost the only one in town, her eyes on Nigel, slumped against the door. Her husband! Dad, I can't explain. I just hope you understand why.

She watched the mayor in the rearview mirror, knowing she had left more of an enemy behind her than she had had and still had no idea why. All she knew was that she wanted out of this town, and this man, a stranger she had just married to save him, might be her ticket for that, for her and her beloved father.

Havan turned to the man in the seat beside her once she was outside of town, pulling over and reaching to feel his forehead. A bad fever, she thought. Lord, we'll need to get that down and fast.

Chapter 2

Struggling under Nigel's height and weight, Havan carefully led him into her cabin. Thank goodness, she thought, he's not overweight. I could never have gotten him in here. She left him leaning against a wall as she quickly threw back covers on a bed before helping him to the edge of the bed and gently shoving him to a sitting position. She reached for his sneakers, pulling them off and setting them aside, a frown on her face for a moment as she studied the mud on them. Something was off about it, she decided. She stood, hands reaching to help him off with his jacket and shirt and then with gentle hands on his t-shirted covered shoulders, she made him lay back on the bed, pulling up blankets on him.

Her hand to his forehead, she frowned. A fever for sure and a high one. Lord, now what? Help me to help him. Don't let him go and die on me, please, dear Lord.

She ran for cold water and clothes, for pain medication, for juice. She worked frantically, trying to reduce his fever, knowing the physician in town would not come out, as much as he would want to. He was tied by the contract he had signed, not knowing that the contract would be held against him, that he was to be the physician for only the people in the town, not the outsiders as they were called. Havan finally drew a breath of relief. The fever seemed to lower. She reached for his hand, feeling a coolness there that had been missing earlier.

She rose, her blue eyes on him, reaching to brush back the dark brown hair, knowing his eyes matched almost exactly the colour. He had opened them once, staring up at her in bewilderment and pain.

She finally turned, seeing for the first time it was night. She was exhausted but knew she needed to eat. She made her tea and then sat, head down on her arms at the kitchen table, her heart in prayer, even though she could not have said what her words were.

She was still there hours later when the door opened and an older man walked in, his steps hesitating as he studied Havan, before he removed his boots, setting them carefully by the door and hanging his jacket and hat up on the rack above them.

He reached for wood to replenish the fire in the stove and then quietly slid the kettle back onto the burner, knowing Havan would want to share a cup of tea with him.

He finally turned, mug in hand, his other hand running down the black curls so much like her mother. Mary, I wish you had lived to see your daughter today. She is such a wonderful young woman. But I hear she's gotten herself into some deep trouble, Lord. We'll be asking your protection on her for that.

Havan stirred, raising her head, turning it to listen for the sounds of Nigel rousing. She frowned, knowing it had been hours since she sat down. She rose, stumbling a bit as she did so, her feet taking her to check on him, finding his fever up but not as bad as it was. She gently raised his head, getting him to swallow more medication, before she stood back, her eyes thoughtful, her mind jumbled.

She returned to the kitchen, her steps stopping as she saw her father standing there, leaning back against the counter, his eyes on his mug.

"Dad? I didn't hear you come in." She was hesitant to speak, not knowing what he had heard. She slid back into the chair, her eyes still on him.

"Havan? Just what did you go and do?" His voice was stern, but she heard the love and concern underneath that.

"I had to, Dad. I couldn't let them do that to him, a complete stranger." Tears lurked beneath the surface.

"I know that, love, but did it have to be you?" He walked around and crouched down beside her, his arm around her. "That's not what a marriage is, you know."

Soberly, she studied her father's face. "I know that, Dad, and it's not what I want. But God told me I had to. He led me across the street and into that room. He didn't have a clue what was going on. He's sick, Dad, sick to the point that he agreed to marry me without knowing exactly what he was doing."

"That's not good, Havan. Not a basis for a marriage." Jackson O'Leary stood, his eyes on his daughter, and then to the bedroom. "You gave him your room?"

"I had to, Dad. He needs a bed, not the couch." She rose, hearing Nigel tossing. "Oh, no! Dad, his fever must be up again. I had a horrible time getting it down in the first place."

Dawn came and with it, a lowering of Nigel's fever. Jackson finally sent his daughter to her rest, telling her to use his bed, he wouldn't be needing it, and then pulling up a chair and watching the young man, seeing something in him that reassured his heart to some extent. He rose, hearing sounds from outside, and sighed. They had arrived, just as he knew they would.

Jackson pulled the weathered wooden door closed behind him, standing back against it, his arms crossed. The men had disturbed the woods around him, quietening the early morning sounds.

"Where is he?" The only officer from town stood in front of him, hand on his weapon, eyes burning a hole into Jackson.

"Nope. Doesn't work that way, Peter. You have no jurisdiction out here and you and the mayor know that only too well."

"He's given me special powers to arrest that man for theft."

Jackson shook his head. "His special powers don't count out here. All of you men know that." He raised his eyes to the other three men flanking Peter, knowing they were on the payroll of the mayor and would not hesitate to use violence to get what they wanted. And this time, they wanted Nigel. Lord, we need some help here.

A sudden clicking turned Peter's head to the side of the cabin and he paled. Havan stood there, her father's rifle pointed at him, dead centre to his chest. He knew the kind of shot she was and that if she wanted to shoot him, he would not walk away from that cabin. Suddenly it just wasn't worth it, the money and the lifestyle he had had. He turned, with a curse, shoving his way past the other men and heading for his car, dirt and stones shooting out behind him as he gunned the motor and headed away as fast as he could.

Jackson tilted his head to watch him go, then turned his attention to the other men, who were trying to keep an eye on both Jackson and Havan.

"Give it up, boys. You can't win this time. And you're trespassing as of now. So toddle off to your homes and tell your boss it won't work. Not this time. Not with us."

They watched the men drive off before Jackson stepped off the porch and approached his daughter, taking the rifle from her.

"Thanks, love. I needed that back up." He peered at her closely and then turned to look behind him. "We're not done with them, not by a long shot."

"No, we're not, Dad. Thank you for sticking up for Nigel, even if you haven't met him yet." She reached to drop a kiss on her father's weathered cheek.

He hugged her, before he turned her to the cabin again. "Go in and check on your man. His fever's been up and down again. I'll make some broth in a while." He watched her walk away, then slowly walked to his thinking post as he called it, a stump set against the back of the cabin. He sank down, weary beyond measure, knowing the fight had just begun, and opened up his heart to God, praying first and longest for his daughter.

Havan hesitated at the bedroom door, her eyes on the back door, knowing her father was there, praying, before she entered the room, to stand and stare at Nigel, who slept, his fever finally broken. She sighed. Lord, what am I to do? What will he say when he realizes what happened? Will he stay or will he run?

As tired as she was, she couldn't think past the thought of him leaving, and not taking her and her father with him. Perhaps this was their chance to escape this town. They hadn't been able to before.

She watched as he turned to his side, and sat beside him, her hand on his shoulder, before she too laid down, sleep claiming her before her head hit the pillow.

Jackson came looking for her later, a small smile on his face as he found her. He reached for a blanket, spreading it over her, before reaching across to feel Nigel's brow. Thank you, Lord. The fever's gone and he's in a natural sleep. Now to face the consequences when he awakes and finds out just how entwined his life has become with ours.

Chapter 3

Shifting his body position, Nigel gradually opened his eyes, blinking in the soft morning light, staring up at an unfamiliar ceiling. He had no idea where he was or even what day it was. He reached to rub at his face, feeling a four-day growth of whiskers and frowned, his gaze stopping as he saw his hand and the ring on it. His heart dropping, he stared at his hand, wondering what he had gone and done that he had no memory of going and doing. He shifted again, feeling a weight on the blankets. Where was he?

His head turning to his side, he froze. Yes, there really was a head there, a head covered in raven-black curls. The young woman was curled up on her side, her left hand on his shoulder, as if to keep contact with him. He saw the matching band on her finger and glanced back at his own hand, holding it up in front of him, trying desperately to remember what had happened and having no idea what had.

Nigel sighed and then prayed. *Lord, what did I do? And where am I? And what happened to those days I seem to have lost?*

He heard the footsteps heading his way, that of an older man, he thought, given the sound of them. His eyes slid closed as he prayed once more. *What is going on, Lord? This is not the vacation I planned on, that's for sure.*

Jackson stood for a moment, his eyes on his beloved daughter, knowing just how bad things could get, and in his heart, thinking that's just what would happen. His eyes raised to the young man and he stepped around the bed.

"Here, there, young fellow. I see you're finally awake."

Nigel nodded wearily, trying to speak. The man he didn't recognize reached to help him sit up, bracing him against the head of the bed, handing him a glass of water.

"Drink this. I'll give you a few moments. Then, we'll need to talk."

Nigel finally shoved the blankets back, his socked feet hitting the floor as he pushed himself to stand, his hand on the wall to brace himself, his hand automatically reaching into his jeans pocket to feel for his phone and wallet. Both were still there. He could feel the weakness in him and knew that something had happened to him, something drastic, but did not know what.

Jackson watched for a moment, then reached for Nigel, an arm around him to help him walk.

"A shower, I'm thinking, young fellow. Havan brought in your bag. Here, brace yourself for a moment against the counter." Jackson was back in less than that, Nigel's bag in his hand. "A shower will help you feel much better. I'll be outside in the kitchen. Call if you need me."

Nigel nodded, almost too weary to speak, as he turned slightly to stare at the closed door. No, he thought, I have no idea where I am or what has happened. Lord, what did I do?

Reaching for a chair back a few minutes later to pull it out from the wooden table, Nigel gratefully sank down, his head in his hands. He sat for a while, his elbows on the table before he sensed someone beside him and looked up. The older man stood here, compassion and worry on his face.

"Here, young fellow. Drink this. I don't know if you drink tea or not, but that's all we have. We can't get any coffee for you, not without going into town, and I'm not prepared to do that, not just yet."

Nigel wrapped his hands around the cup, grateful for the warmth.

"What happened? And where am I?"

When he received no response, he looked up, to see the older man standing at the counter, his eyes on the bedroom door, a worried look flitting across his face.

Nigel turned slightly as he heard a sound from that way and watched as the young woman moved towards him, her hand going to feel his forehead before she walked past him and hugged the man, reaching then for a mug of tea and sliding into a chair across from him. Her eyes studied him, he saw, and then drew him in. They reminded him of a summer's sky, the dark blue that comes near the end of a day.

"How are you feeling now?" Her voice was low, melodious.

He shrugged. "I have no idea how I'm supposed to feel. Can someone explain to me exactly what's going on and why I am wearing this?" He held up his hand, the band sparkling in the sunlight streaming through the kitchen window. He sighed to himself.

"I'm sorry. I didn't mean to bite. I am just so confused right now."

"And it's understandable." The man reached and pulled back a chair beside the young woman, his hand lightly resting on her head for a moment before he sat. "My name is Jackson O'Leary, and this is my daughter, Havan." He tilted his head to look at his daughter. When she didn't speak, he shook his head. "Havan. You are going to have to explain, you know. You've had four days to avoid doing just that."

"I know, Dad. I know. I just don't know how to explain."

"Then explain. Now." Nigel was beginning to feel angry and used. His face grew stern, a look his friends knew meant he had been pushed to his limit.

"I'm sorry. I did the only thing I could think of to help you. God was there that day, Nigel." Havan's voice was low, almost inaudible. "Here in Sanctuary, we have a mayor who is heavily into crime. We can't get anyone to come in and deal with him. Part of his mandate has been to see his four daughters marry. To do this, he brought in a law that says he can marry any unattached male that enters Sanctuary to one of them, unless that male agrees to marry someone else. He had planned that for you, Nigel. You don't know his daughters. You would have been trapped into a life that would have killed you eventually.

"God was there that day. I watched them take you into the city hall. You were sick. When I talked to you, you could barely put a sentence together." She sighed, her eyes on her father as he nodded. "I asked if you had a wife or a girlfriend. When you say no, I asked if you would marry me. I couldn't explain at that point. No one could." She shuddered, then studied her hands. "I just had to." She rose, tears blinding her eyes as she ran from the cabin, the door thudding closed behind her.

Nigel sat in shock, not sure he had heard her correctly, his eyes on the door. Looking at Jackson, he saw the nod and the sorrow on his face.

"He does that?"

Jackson gave a grim smile. "Let's put it this way, he tries. He's never been able to make it happen. Young men avoid this town. Word has gotten around the area. If one of the outsiders or someone from another town sees a young stranger heading this way, they stop him and send him on a different route."

"And I didn't get stopped. Or maybe I did. I stopped outside of town to check a tire and almost got run down." Nigel sat back, scrubbing his hand down his face, before he stopped, his hand on his chest. "And now I have to wonder why."

"You do. As Havan says, Nigel, she felt she had to step in. She's not impulsive, not by any means." Jackson stood and paced, before spinning to stare at him. "I won't have her hurt, young man."

Nigel nodded, feeling suddenly fatigued. "I understand. I will do my best."

"See that you do. And just keep in mind, sometimes your best won't be good enough. I just pray that it is." Jackson turned to stare at the door. "I'm not sure what your plans are or where you live, but it's going to be extremely difficult to get you out of here now. Our main way out is through town. The mayor has already tried to arrest you, but we've stopped him."

"Then, I guess we have some plans to make." Nigel yawned, fatigue claiming his body. "I'm sorry. I don't know why I am so tired."

"You've been sick with a fever. We've had to do some hard work to bring it down." Jackson stared at the door, before heading for it. "I'll be right back. Havan needs to be here."

"Jackson, wait. Did you call her Havan?"

Jackson paused, knowing that he needed to talk to Nigel, but worried about his daughter. "Havan. She's named after my grandmother. And that was a lady to be reckoned with."

Nigel waited but Jackson didn't continue, instead heading out the door. Nigel sighed. *Lord, I have no idea what's coming and I'm not sure I want to. But so far, it looks as if You've brought me here, allowed what happened to happen, and now I need to know where I go from here.*

Havan looked up from the garden she had stooped to weed, finally standing and wiping the dirt from her hands. "Dad?"

"You need to face him, Havan. You can't hide." He was stern, he knew, but he also knew he had to be. Havan had been sheltered a good portion of her life, and now was facing something no one should have to face.

"I know, Dad. I just don't know how to explain it to him." She studied the surrounding trees, listening to the sounds of nature and then slowly turning in a circle. "Someone's out there, Dad."

"There is. They have been since you brought that young man home. I'm afraid for you, Havan. I have no idea how far he'll go." He reached to hug his daughter, before turning her and arm around her shoulders, directing her back to the cabin. "I have wanted for years to get you out of here, Havan. You're a danger to the mayor, just why, I haven't yet figured out." He nodded towards the cabin. "This may be God's way of doing just that. I just wish you hadn't jumped in like you did."

She didn't say anything, just opened the door and stood, watching Nigel, as head down on his arms, he slept. She sighed. That talk they needed had just been postponed, just as she was geared up to face him. She walked past, reaching for a blanket and then gently covering him with it, her hand lingering for a moment on his head, a prayer raising within her.

Lord, I have no idea what's next. He's angry and he has every right to be. Coming through Sanctuary changed his life in a way no one's life should be changed.

Chapter 4

Rising later that day from the table, Nigel stretched, feeling somewhat stronger. He stared down at where he had been sitting, then at the window. He had been there for hours, he thought, and hadn't heard anyone moving around him. He reached for the blanket, pausing for a moment to feel its softness, wondering where it had come from and who had covered him, and then folded it, walking back through to the other room and setting it neatly on a chair. He slowly turned, searching the room, studying it, trying to determine where he was. He had no idea.

A sound from the kitchen caught his attention and had him heading that way, pausing as he reached it. Havan stood at the sink, her head bent over the vegetables she had brought in. He knew she was aware he was behind her. He could tell by her stance.

"I'm sorry. I wasn't very nice early." Nigel waited, his eyes on Havan, not quite sure how to talk to her. He had never found it easy to converse with girls or ladies, except those of his own family and a couple of close friends.

She nodded, her hands stilling for a moment, before she turned the water on, cutting off any chance of conversation. Nigel grinned to himself. Avoidance, he thought. Just what he would do.

He finally moved to stand beside her, leaning against the counter. "Havan? We need to talk."

She finally sighed, looking up and out the window at the gathering dusk. "We do, Nigel. I'm sorry. It's the only thing I could think of to save you. You can have the marriage annulled once you're away from here." She turned to walk away, his hand on her forearm stopping her movement.

"No. Do not walk away from me again. Stay and talk to me. Running won't help." He waited as she finally nodded, turning to face him, devastation on her face. "I understand why you felt you had to step in. I thank you for that. I just don't understand how a man has that much power."

She snorted in a very unladylike manner. "That's who he is. He took over the town twenty-five years ago. He's all my generation have known. The families make sure the young men are gone by the time they turn eighteen. Some of them have never seen or heard from them again. They're too afraid to have them come back."

"That's just not right. No man should have that power." Nigel stared down at the floor for a moment, his eyes following the herringbone pattern on the wood. "How do we stop him?"

Havan paused, reaching for a towel to dry her hands before hanging it back up on the wall. "That's just it, Nigel. We have no idea how to stop him. We don't have the modern conveniences I am sure you're used to. We know you have a phone, but you'll not likely get reception. Not where the cabin is."

"Then I find somewhere that I can get reception." His phone in his hand, he stared at it. "I have some bars. I can likely get out a text to a friend."

Her hand on his stopped his fingers on the keyboard. "Wait, Nigel. We have to plan this. We can't have any of your friends just walking into that town. They'll face the same thing you did."

He sighed, staring down at his phone and then up at her face, seeing her sincerity and worry about his friends. He slid his phone away. "Yeah, you're probably right.

But we need to get out of here." He began to pace, lost in thought.

Havan leaned against the counter for a few moments watching him before she turned back to her supper preparations. "We can't get out from here, Nigel. At least, not on the road. There is only one way out from here that you could use your truck, and that takes you right through town. That won't work. They'll be watching for you."

"And I don't get why. I'm already married." He smirked as he held up his hand, studying the ring. "This is not that nice a ring. Not what you would have picked out. And yours is not what I would have chosen for you."

She stared at him in disbelief before she stared to laugh, drawing a frown from him before he grinned. "The mayor picked those out for his daughter. The one who was on her way to marry you."

Nigel began to laugh at that. "Well, then, we'll do something about these when we get away from here." He paced again, not seeing her look of shock and then her narrowed eyes assessing him.

New rings, she thought? What is going on here, Lord? I have no idea where You're taking us.

Nigel spun, walking back to stand in front of her, his hands opening and closing before he finally placed them on her upper arms. "Havan? I can't get used to that name. I love it. It suits you. Now where was I?" He stared down at her, lost in her beauty, before she poked him in the chest.

"You're standing in my kitchen, buster, keeping me from getting supper. But what are your thoughts? Have you an idea of how to get away?"

"I'm working on one." He walked to the open door, staring off towards the horizon. "How far is it to the next town?"

"By road, about twenty miles. Why?"

"What about cross country?"

Jackson spoke from behind him. "Maybe ten, as the crow flies. But it's a rough country, lots of hills and ups and downs. Are you thinking of heading that way?"

Nigel turned, catching the older man's speculative look and then cast a quick glance at Havan, who worked away, her back to him, but he could tell she was listening. "Maybe. It's something to think about, don't you?"

Jackson nodded. "I've done that trip many times. So has Havan. It's not something you can just take off and walk. You need to plan for it."

"Then maybe we should start planning." Nigel walked over and took the plates out of Havan's hands, setting them on the table and then searching for the utensil drawer. "We may have to. This man has to be stopped. I don't want anyone else hurt, not the way he's hurt Havan."

Jackson gave a slow nod, before he walked over to the stove, shoving the kettle onto a burner, moving the meat around in the frying pan. He shot a quick look at Havan, a frown on his face for a moment. *Lord, what is going on here? Havan's different tonight, and I think it's because of that young man over there. She's not been around men of her age in recent years and that makes me concerned. Yes, I know he's likely a good man, but we don't know much about him and that too is concerning to me.*

Spinning around from the door he had gone back to, Nigel paced into the living room, his eyes searching it. He saw the little homey touches that Havan likely had put around. He frowned. *Where were the photos of the family? Of her growing up? Of her parents?* He turned to find Jackson standing near him.

"Your photos, Jackson?"

Jackson shook his head, sorrow briefly crossing his face. "We don't have any, Nigel. We don't have the money for that and this new-fangled digital stuff doesn't work here. We have to watch our electricity. We have solar power but it has to be used wisely."

Nigel nodded, saddened at the thought that Havan had no pictures of her childhood or youth. "What about your wife?"

Jackson sighed, a look crossing his face that Nigel couldn't place, before he turned and walked away, shoulders slumped, leaving the younger man staring after him. Nigel heard the back door close softly.

Havan appeared at his side, a hand on his arm. "Nigel? What did you ask Dad? I haven't seen him look like that before."

"I just asked about your mother." He stared down at her, seeing sorrow in her eyes.

"Oh, Nigel. You didn't know." She drew him back and to a seat on the couch, her hand on his, trying to find the words she needed. "No, you wouldn't have known. Mom died when I was about two months old. She got really sick and Dad tried to get the doctor to come out to see her. When he wouldn't, he tried to get her into town and was barred by the mayor's men. She died in his arms two days later." She stared at the floor. "What no one ever knew until then and the doctor himself hadn't fully understood from his contract was that he could only treat the people in town. None of us outsiders could be under his care. It broke the doctor, Nigel. He just shrivelled up and died inside when he realized what had happened. He never knew Dad tried to get to him."

"The mayor again, I take it?" At her nod, he shook his head. "Again, how does he have that much power?" He rose and walked to the fireplace, staring down at the cold hearth. "He has to have someone backing him. That's the only explanation." He spun. "I need his full name." He pulled out his phone. "I have some bars. I'm sending off a text to a friend."

"Just please be careful. We can't have them coming into town. Who knows what his men will do? They're after you." She sighed, her eyes on the floor, her hands rubbing against one another.

"And you. He'll be after you, Havan." Sitting back beside her, Nigel reached to still her hands, his hand strong and warm on hers. "We need to protect you. Your father can't lose another lady in his life."

He reached for his phone, tapping quickly and then sending a message off to his friends. He hadn't told Havan or Jackson yet what his employment was. That question had just not come up, but he knew it would eventually, and he would have to confess. Now, his main thought was on how to get Havan away from the town and to safety. He knew she was in grave danger, and he wanted to save her. He knew his four friends would be there as soon as they could, with all the information they could find out. A plan would likely already be in place, if he knew them at all.

Havan watched him closely, studying him now that he was up and about, finding him fascinating. She sighed. He would be gone shortly, she just knew it. Once he was out of danger, he would leave and that she decided she didn't like at all. Lord, what am I to do? I know he'll leave, but I pray that I'll have peace when he does. Guide us both, dear Lord. I don't even know if he believes in You, and taking that step the other day really didn't go with my profession of faith, now did it?

Chapter 5

Reaching for his phone, Nigel quickly scrolled through his messages, a sigh of relief coming from him. He knew that his friends would be concerned and would head his way as soon as they could. He responded, letting them know exactly where he was but also with a warning not to go through the town.

He turned from the door to find Jackson watching him, an unreadable look on his face. Nigel approached him, sliding back a chair from the other side of the table, before seating himself, setting his phone on the table in front of him.

"Nigel? What are you up to?" Jackson got right to the point, a forefinger pointing at his phone.

"I've asked my friends for help. They're working on something and will get back to me. They want us to leave, if we can."

"That's something I've considered for years. The Lord has just never told me to go." He paused, his eyes on Nigel, before he looked down. "That is, until now. Nigel, I am going to be bold. I don't want my daughter hurt any more than she has been already by this situation with the mayor. I know you had no part of it, not at first. Now, I need to know. Where do you stand with God?" Jackson watched the younger man, seeing the whiteness of his face and the dark circles under his eyes and knew he should be letting him go to his rest, but needing some answers first.

Nigel had waited, wondering if this was where Jackson had been headed. Had the roles been reversed, he would have asked the question a lot sooner. He watched closely as Jackson stared at the table, a worried look crossing his face.

"You're worried about Havan and you have every right to be. She took a step she shouldn't have had to take. No young woman should have had to step in like that. We need to do something about that man." Nigel tamped down the rising anger he felt. "Yes, Jackson, I am a Christian, believing with every fibre of my being in God, Jesus and what the Bible stands for. Does that answer your question?"

Jackson sat back, relief in his heart, but not on his face. He didn't know Nigel well enough for that, not yet. "It does, Nigel. I just pray you mean what you say. If you don't, you'll answer to me." He rose, coming around the table to lay a hand on Nigel's shoulder. "Take my bed tonight, Nigel. Havan's already asleep."

"I can't take your bed, Jackson. You need it."

Jackson shook his head, even as he rose and came around the table and hauled Nigel to his feet. "Go on, Nigel. I won't be sleeping for a while, not tonight. That couch in there and I are old friends."

Nigel studied him for a moment before he nodded wearily and headed for the bedroom. Jackson stood where he was, watching as Nigel paused at Havan's bedroom door, his hand resting on it as he bowed his head before he moved on, staggering somewhat in his fatigue. He watched as Nigel stopped at the watercolour on the wall, a finger coming up to touch a spot on it before he moved on to Jackson's bedroom and disappeared.

Jackson walked to the wall, studying the painting, knowing exactly what Nigel had seen. He had painted that when Havan had been small and had put her into the picture, a little waif in the midst of the meadow flowers.

He sighed as he turned, heading for the outdoors and his workshop. He had things he had to tend to, he knew, that would prepare him to leave this place of his, where he had brought his bride and then buried her. He prayed for the younger couple, for his daughter especially, as he feared for what they would be facing. He turned from his work after a while, reaching instead for the Bible he kept in his shop, finding his chair and then searching for the passages he wanted. How did Sanctuary ever become what it is, Lord? I look at the sanctuary cites of the Old Testament. That's what my Emily and I were searching for. I would have gladly moved for her, but she wanted to live here. To raise our family in a small town.

Chapter 6

Turning from her garden, Havan searched the woods around her. It had gotten too still, she thought. There should be the chatter of birds and squirrels, the sound of insects, the rustling of small animals she always heard. She spun in a circle, and then turned to run for the house, fear at her heels, knowing that someone was out there and she had reason to fear. Her heart pounded in her ears in time with the speed of her feet hitting the path.

Nigel looked up from the wood he was splitting at the sound of the running feet and dropped the axe, heading for Havan.

"Havan?"

"In the house. Now. Nigel." She grabbed his hand, pulling him with her, slamming the door and shoving the bolts home before running for the front door and doing the same.

Nigel stood, shock on his face. "Havan? What is going on?"

"Someone is out there, Nigel. I don't know who but I can tell you I have never felt fear like that before. Never ever. Not in my whole life." She stood, hands on her face, her eyes huge with fright.

"Where's your rifle?"

"You're not going out there, Nigel. These men are vicious."

"I know that. I know how to take care of myself." He turned, searching for the rifle and not seeing it. "Where is it?"

"Dad has it with him." She caught his arm, spinning him back to face her. "And just how do you know how to take care of yourself?"

"We've never talked, and we should have. Has it only been three days since I woke up here, married to someone I don't know and not knowing when or how I can leave?" Nigel tamped down his anger, knowing it was not directed at Havan. "I work in security, Havan. As in protecting people. That's my job."

"Security? As in bodyguard?" Her eyes grew round at the thought. "God be praised. You're just who we need." She turned, heading for a window to peek out. "I don't see anyone. But someone was out there. I could sense them. The woods were too quiet."

"Yes, in a way, I am. My brothers do that part of our business. But that's not what I do. I do security systems, installing them." He drew her away from the window. "You need to stay away from the windows, Havan. Please. Now, where is your Dad?"

She shrugged. "He headed out sometime last night. I have no idea where. He does that every once in a while." She spun as she heard steps on the back porch and then a light tap.

Nigel was at the door ahead of her, waiting as she listened and hearing the word she wanted to hear, opened the door and drew her father in. Nigel nodded to himself, glad they had set up a safe program such as that.

Jackson reached to pull his daughter into a hard hug. "I prayed you were here, Havan. I was so scared when I saw your basket and the men's tracks. They were after you this time, love. They wanted you. I heard them leaving and overheard a bit of their conversation." He set her back from him, his hands on her shoulders before he looked at Nigel, standing close behind her. "Nigel, we need to make some plans. We need to get Havan out of here. You, too."

Nigel nodded. "I know. I've been trying to figure out a plan. Do you have a map of the area?"

Jackson nodded. "This way. I don't leave it out as a general rule." He headed for the desk in the living room. "It's here in the desk. We can spread it out on the kitchen table. It's a topographical one a friend made me."

Nigel stood and stared at the map, seeing how much detail was on it. "This is good. Whoever did it did a wonderful job on it." He stared up at Jackson. "Okay. Show me exactly where we are and where we would have to walk out."

Jackson complied, his finger tracing the route, his voice quiet and confident as he spoke. "It would take a good day to walk out."

Nigel nodded. "Okay. So we'll plan for that then. When?"

"The sooner the better, I think." Jackson looked up at Havan standing beside him. "Havan?" When she didn't respond, he touched her arm lightly, causing her to jump. "Havan? You need to pack what we talked about. Can you do that?"

She nodded, her eyes on the map. "Dad. They'll expect us to take our usual route. You know right well they've tracked us more than once."

Jackson sighed at that. "I know they have. But what other route is there?"

"The deer trail. It's a bit longer, but we could do it. We've have to plan to stay out over night. There are the caves about halfway there."

Jackson nodded, a thoughtful look on his face. "That might work."

Nigel spoke. "Show me exactly what you mean."

She pointed out an alternative route. He watched her finger move along the map and then reached to stop her.

"What about this?" He traced his own finger along another route. "What is this like?"

Jackson shook his head. "It's dangerous, Nigel. Lots of loose rocks. Debris. Downed trees. That area takes the brunt of any storms we have. It is possible though. I walked part of it in the early summer."

"And that is one route they would not expect us to take." Nigel walked away, hands jammed into his jeans pockets, lost in thought.

Jackson turned to Havan, his mouth open to speak before he snapped it closed, seeing the look in her eyes as she watched Nigel. He nodded. *It's happening, Mary. Our little girl is falling in love, and I just wish you were here to walk with her through this. I don't have a clue what to do. We miss you.* He blinked rapidly to clear the tears away before he turned her to face her bedroom.

"Go on, Havan. Pack your stuff. We'll be leaving in the morning, early."

She nodded. "Dad, what about your paintings?"

"I've put them somewhere safe. Take a look around, Havan. They're not here any more."

She stared at the walls, seeing the empty spots, sadness filling her. "I see that, Dad. I hate this."

"So do I. We have no choice now. I have to get you to safety. I don't want you in their hands." He nodded towards Nigel, his voice lowering. "And I don't want Nigel to confront them. It won't go well."

She sighed. "I know, Dad. He told me today he's in security, setting up systems. He didn't say much more than that."

"He doesn't need to, love. I know his character. He will do everything he can to keep you safe. Now, go. Do what I've asked." Jackson watched her walk away, realizing that he had likely overstepped his bounds in asking that. Even married in such a manner as she had been, she was someone's wife and it was her husband's responsibility to ask that of her.

"Nigel?" Jackson turned as he heard Nigel approaching.

"What else do we need to do? I see you've cleared the memories away." Nigel's keen eyes had spotted the missing pictures. "I take it they were your work?" At Jackson's reluctant nod, Nigel gave a quick grin. "I recognized them. My parents have three of your paintings. I am honoured to meet you, sir."

Jackson waved away Nigel's words. "Not now. We need to pack food stuff. If we leave in the middle of the night, take the usual trail, we can cut off to the deer trail and then cut off from it to the other trail."

"Okay, so it's what now, mid afternoon? What time do you think to leave? Real early morning?"

Jackson gave a quick grin even as he shook his head. "You think too fast for my old brain, Nigel. I would say about 3 in the morning. There should be enough light to let us head out on the regular trail. About two hours in, we shoot off onto the deer trail. It's hard to find. If we're careful, our footprints won't give us away."

Nigel nodded, frowning as he felt his phone vibrating. He pulled it out, staring at it. "I'll need to charge this before we leave. My truck?"

"I would suggest we move it to the end of the laneway and park it there, hood out. That may buy us some time. If we move it just before we leave, it will draw their attention that way, hopefully pulling all them to it. Is it important to you?"

Nigel shook his head. "No, not really. It's just an old one I picked up and tinkered with, not wanting to drive my usual vehicle on this trip. It was supposed to be a relaxing, stress free getaway."

Jackson began to laugh. "Stress free? Relaxing? Can't say as we have had that for you, now have we?" He nodded at his phone. "Plug that in somewhere and let it charge."

Nigel nodded absentmindedly, his eyes on a message. "Just great."

"Nigel?"

He looked up at Jackson's question and shook his head. "I have people out there somewhere trying to find me. Just what we needed. They're coming in on a trail, likely the one we want to head out on."

"Tell them to act as if they're lost or something. We don't need any more complications." Jackson turned as he heard Havan approaching.

"Havan, make up the bread into sandwiches and get the water bottles ready. We'll have a good meal tonight before we head out." He nodded at Nigel who was engrossed in his message. "He's got people heading this way. We don't know them. I'm sure they're fine and trustworthy, but watch yourself. For now, stick close to either Nigel or myself."

"I understand, Dad. But I highly doubt they'll be a problem." She turned and headed for the kitchen, pulling out the bread and the meat from the fridge. "Dad, what about the veggies and the garden?"

"Leave the veggies in the fridge. Earl will stop by and check on the cabin for us. He'll take them."

She stared at him. "That's where you were. Thank you." She reached to hug her father, before her eyes tracked to Nigel. "What about Nigel, Dad? Is he up to the trek out?"

"I don't know, love. He'll have to be. We can't carry him if he's not."

She nodded, her eyes thoughtful as she turned back to the counter, freezing as she looked out the window. "Dad? Who are those men? I've never seen them around again."

He moved to stand behind her, one arm around her shoulder. "I would say that's Nigel's cavalry, riding in to the rescue." He turned to find Nigel, seeing him at his shoulder. "Do you know these men, Nigel?"

Nigel sighed. "Unfortunately I do. My two brothers and one of my brothers-in-law, riding in to the rescue as they say." He looked at Jackson, then tilted his head to watch Havan's face. "We need to be very cautious. We can't let the men watching us know they are friends."

Jackson soon his head. "No, we can't. That would bring in a huge complication we don't need and put your family at risk." He turned to head for the door as he heard a call from one of the men. "Stay put." He pointed to where Nigel had set his phone to charge. "Bring them up to speed on the plan. Tell them to act as strangers to you, too. Hopefully you don't look too much like them."

Nigel began to laugh, bringing their eyes to him. "Sorry. We do look enough alike Mom had trouble telling us apart when we were kids. She still does at times."

"That's not what I wanted to hear, Nigel!" Jackson hesitated at the door. "This is where we'll need to pray and pray hard, Nigel. It's only going to be God that gets us out of here."

Nigel stood back from the door as he heard Jackson talking with the three men before the door opened and Jackson entered, followed by Nigel's brothers. He shook his head, a small grin playing around his face.

"Just couldn't stay away, now could you?"

Nevin, Nigel's older brother, had been looking around the kitchen, finally setting his gaze on Nigel. "Heard you got yourself into a predicament and needing rescuing."

Nigel laughed at his nonsense before he reached to hug him, turning to hug his other brother, Nolan, and his sister's husband, Brett. "Sure. Come when we already have a plan in place to get out."

Nolan had turned to Jackson, asking questions in a rapid-fire manner, causing Jackson to frown and then smile. Yes, he thought, these men will definitely work out a plan to get us out of here. It will be interesting to see what happens. His eyes searched for Havan, not seeing her, and knowing that she would have tucked herself somewhere safe for now, until she knew the men were to be trusted.

Brett stood at the counter, studying the sandwich preparation and then just continuing on from what Havan had left. He tucked the sandwiches into the fridge before reaching for the kettle. His hand went next into his pack, pulling out coffee.

"Nigel, do you know if there's a coffee pot here?"

Nigel shrugged, his eyes on Jackson. "I doubt it very much, Brett. We drink tea in this cabin."

Brett spun, mouth open, as he stared at Nigel before catching the narrow-eyed look Nevin was shooting his brother, before he nodded. Interesting. A diehard coffee drinker switched to tea. Has to be a woman involved and if what he's told Nolan was correct, there is. He searched the room, not seeing anyone other than the men.

Jackson dug into the back of a cupboard to pull out an old coffeepot. "Here, young fellow. Let me. I think I can still remember how to make coffee. It's been a couple of years since we've had any. We only buy what we can pack in, going to Sanctuary as little as possible."

Nevin paced the kitchen, hands locked behind his back. "That's what I don't get. How does he have that much control?"

Jackson shrugged. "Because he does. Because the people have let him. His men have terrorized anyone who has stood up to him." He pointed at Nigel. "He's after him right now."

"Yeah, we kinda of figured that one out. But why?" Nolan spoke from where he had sat at the table. He was the youngest of the three brothers.

"Because I thwarted his plans." Nigel shook his head at the question on Nolan's face. "I'll explain later. Right now, we need to formalize our plans. We're leaving here tonight."

"That's what we thought. We left our vehicles in the town you're heading for." Nevin pulled out a chair and sat, his eyes on Nigel. He gave a quiet thanks to Brett for the mug of coffee set in front of him.

Jackson finally sat down himself, his hands wrapped around his mug of tea, a sudden chill running through him. He knew God was working but he still couldn't see how they would ever make it out, unhurt or even alive. The mayor was that deadly.

He spoke quietly for a few minutes, giving the history of the town and what had transpired in the last few years. He finally raised his eyes to Nigel, finding Nigel's gaze on his mug, an unreadable look on his face.

Nigel looked up at a soft sound from Nolan, who sat across from him and heard his quiet comment.

"And who do we have here, Nigel?" Nolan's gaze was directed past Nigel, towards the living room.

Nigel turned partway in his chair to look behind him and then rose, heading for Havan, who had appeared in the living room.

Nigel's brothers turned to watch him, before their eyes saw the look on Jackson's face. They shared a glance and then turned back to their plans, knowing Nigel would introduce them when he was ready.

Chapter 7

Standing in front of Havan, Nigel ducked his head to look at her face, seeing her hesitation and the fear she felt. He finally sighed, reaching to draw her to him into a tight hug. She resisted but he refused to let her go, finally feeling her relax against him and hug him back.

"Are you okay?" His voice was barely above a whisper.

She shook her head. "I'm scared, Nigel. And I have never been scared like this ever before in my life. Something is about to happen, and it will be bad."

"I know, love. I know. We'll do our best to keep you safe." He turned his head for a moment to stare back at his brothers, finding Nolan's speculative glance on him. "Listen, I need you to meet my family. They've come in to help get us out."

"Are they the ones in security?"

"They are. Nevin heads up our company. Nolan heads up our protective services branch. Brett is our computer expert. They won't bite."

"I know that. It's just…" Her voice died away.

"It's just what we went through, how we met, how we're tied to one another. Is that it?" When she nodded, he hugged her tight to him again, his head dropping to the top of hers. "I promise, my love. They will understand totally why you did what you did. It's how they are. Even Brett will understand."

He finally turned her to face the kitchen, his arm tight around her, and led her to the doorway. Her father was on his feet, his eyes on her as they approached, worry on his face. The other men rose.

Havan drew herself closer to Nigel, seeing the height of the men and their dark colouring, fear flowing through her for a moment. His arm tightened around her as he dropped his head to study her face, waiting until she looked up at him before he nodded.

"Guys. This is Havan. She's Jackson's daughter." He paused, his eyes on her face, waiting until she looked up at him again and shook her head. He sighed. He would go along with her for now, but his brothers were too astute. It would not be long before they noticed the rings and questioned him. "She's the one who found me in Sanctuary and rescued me."

The other men greeted her, then returned to their seats, throwing glances at Nigel before they exchanged looks amongst themselves. There was more to the story, they knew, but they also knew they could not push Nigel. He would just shutter himself and not say a word. That was how he was.

Nigel worked with Havan as she prepared their meal, quiet words spoken infrequently between them, as he listened to the plans being made. Her saw her freeze as she looked out the window and moved to watch.

"Jackson? Who's that?"

Jackson was on his feet, his hands reaching for his rifle as he made his way to the door. "You young men stay in here, unless I run into difficulty. We don't want them to know you're related to Nigel. It will mean an all out war if I know the mayor."

Jackson stood in front of the cabin, his rifle across his chest as he listened to the men before he pointed it to the sky and fired it, causing the men in front of him to jump, stare at him and then turn and almost run from him.

Jackson waited for a few minutes before he came back in.

"Dad? Was that them again?" Havan was at his side, drawn tight to him in a hug for a moment.

"It was, love. They brought an ultimatum. You and Nigel are to report to town tomorrow morning. Apparently, the mayor has decided there were irregularities the other day." He stopped, biting off his words as he watched Havan's face.

She broke out into disbelieving laughter. "Irregularities? Oh, my! What next from him?" She turned to find Nigel, her eyes on his, seeing his understanding in them.

"Come on, Havan. Let's get these men fed. We'll shelter them for the night and then send them on their way in the morning." Jackson watched her until she nodded.

"Sure, Dad. Let's feed our guests. It looks like rain out there, doesn't it? We can't have them sleeping out in the elements. If they would like to stay, our living room floor is not that uncomfortable, or so I'm told."

Jackson stared at her for a moment, not sure where she was going with her words before he nodded, catching her glance towards the window. He thought he had heard a sound outside the window.

"I think that's a good idea, love. How be you and Nigel finish off the meal. Nevin, is it? Come with me. We'll need some more wood for the stove." Jackson had his hand on Nevin's arm, pointing to the back door, even as Brett was heading for the front door.

A yell came from outside and Nolan spun, not sure where to go. A few minutes later, Brett came back in, laughing hard.

"Your father's something else, Havan. He caught one of the men eavesdropping. Scared him good, I think. He took off, white as a sheet."

Havan laughed. "That would be Dad." She turned back to the sink, the sun reflecting off her ring as she raised her hand to tuck a lock of hair behind her ear, catching Nolan's eye.

Nolan frowned, turning to say something to Nigel, catching him rubbing at his face, the ring on his finger shining bright in the sun. A confused look on his face, he stalked over to his brother, a hand coming out to grip his wrist and stop the movement of his hand and to pull it away from his face.

"Nigel? Just what is going on here? Just what do you go and do? You didn't have this before you left home. You wouldn't do this to Mom and Dad or any of the rest of us. As far as we knew, you never dated. Anyone."

Nigel sighed, his eyes on his younger brother, sensing Nevin beside him, before his gaze raised to Havan, who had spun at Nolan's words, her hands on her mouth, her eyes huge. He broke free, moving to stand in front of her and shield her from the other men. He knew Brett had flanked Nolan. It's what he did. Jackson had stayed by the door after setting the rifle on the rack, his eyes on his daughter, frustration and concern on his face.

His hands on hers where she still rested them on her cheeks, Nigel studied Havan. "We have to tell them, love. There's no way around it."

She nodded, her eyes finally raised to his, seeing the compassion and caring there before she frowned. He had something else in his eyes, a look similar to one she had seen on occasion in her father's when he spoke of her mother. That gave her hope that her feelings might just be returned. She knew she was falling in love with him, but would not tell him that, not wanting to trap him in something he might wish to escape.

"Nigel? Care to explain?" Nigel heard the concerned big brother tone in Nevin's voice.

He turned, his arms going around Havan, to keep her by his side. He just knew she'd run if she could and he had no intention of that happening.

"What would you like me to explain, Nevin? That I was really sick when I reached Sanctuary? That someone had tried to sabotage my truck to stop me from getting to town? That the mayor tried to marry me off to a daughter of his? That a beautiful young woman stepped in, somehow got me to agree to marry her, and then did just that, throwing herself into danger as she did so and in doing so, ruined any chance she had of being wooed and courted before marriage as she rightly deserves? What more would you like to know that we can talk about later?" Anger tinged Nigel's voice as he thought through what had happened. It shouldn't have, should it, Lord. Now what? How do I face the rest of my family?

Nevin began waving his hands in the air before Nigel had finished, a shocked look on his face. "Wait a minute, Nige. There is no way that happens. Not in this day and age."

Havan struggled to escape from Nigel, frustration on her face. His arms tightened on her and his face bent to her ear as he whispered to her, stilling her movements and turning her face to his, as she watched him closely before nodding. Nigel raised his head to face his family again.

"It does happen, Nevin. If you were to go to town, you would find very few young men our age or younger. They send them away before they turn 18, just to prevent this from happening. The mayor has a law, and we're not even sure how legal it is, that any single male entering Sanctuary has to marry one of his daughters." He grinned suddenly as he looked at Jackson. "Jackson, what was to happen if all four were married? They couldn't marry more than one."

Jackson started to laugh. "Now that's a question I'm not sure anyone has ever asked. I don't think we want to know the answer." He turned to Nevin, compassion on his face as he saw the shock on his and the other men's faces. "My daughter has placed herself in danger, willingly and at God's leading, I might add, to save your brother. We fought a fever in him for four days, he was that sick. He would never have known what had happened if Havan had not stepped in, just awakened, trapped in a marriage he didn't want. He also would never have been able to leave town. The mayor would have seen to that."

Nevin stood, watching Nigel as he stared back at him. He heard the murmurs between Brett and Nolan, knowing they were waiting for him to make a movement. Lord, I have to do this right. I only get one chance and if I do it wrong, it will hurt my brother and the young lady who reached out to him. He stepped forward, stopping in front of Havan. He felt Nigel's eyes boring into him, a warning deep in them. He sighed to himself. I know, Nigel, I know, he muttered to himself. Just let me do this, okay?

His hand on to Havan's upper arm, he paused, his eyes on hers, seeing the apprehension and fear in them. He bent, dropping a kiss to her cheek.

"Welcome to the family, Havan. We're glad to have you as one of us." He heard her faint sigh of relief and felt Nigel's hand on his shoulder before he stepped back, letting Nolan and Brett make their own welcome. He moved to stand near Jackson.

"You know, this may not be a legal marriage." Jackson had concerns about that.

"Brett was muttering something on our walk here. I think he checked out something he wanted to talk to Nigel about before he shared with us."

Brett had looked up at those words and nodded. "It's legal. Whether the law is legal or not, this marriage is. The minister registered it right away, likely to prevent the mayor from declaring it invalid. Nigel asked me to check to see if it had been registered, but asked that I not say anything until he could explain to you what happened."

"Well, that's that, then." Jackson shared a look with his daughter, sorrow briefly flickering in his gaze. "This is not how these two young people should have married. They should have been able to meet their life mates, court, and then marry."

"No, it's not." Nevin paced, anger simmering just below the surface. He remembered how he had met and wooed his own wife, the excitement and anticipation of starting a life together, the love that had developed so strongly before they married. He knew it had been like that for his sisters and Nolan. He had wanted that for Nigel. Now, that would never happen. He knew his brother well enough to know he would never walk away from Havan, not matter what happened.

"Nevin, don't go there." Nigel's low words beside him startled him, then had him turning to his brother. "It will be okay. Really, it will. God has led this so far. Let Him lead us the rest of the way."

Nevin drew his brother away from the others and into the living room, his eyes on his brother's face. "You've fallen in love with her, haven't you? No. Don't say anything. She needs to hear it first from you. I know you only too well. I can see that in you."

Nigel nodded, sorrow on his face. "It's just too wrong, Nevin. We need to stop him somehow, and I don't know how we can. I suspect he has someone behind him." He turned so he could watch Havan interacting with his brother and brother-in-law, hearing her soft laugh at the teasing Nolan was doing. "Nolan's taken with her. That's good. He'll help her to fit into the family." He sighed. "I just don't know what Mom and Dad will say. And then we have Nora and Noelle to deal with."

"Nora and Noelle will just welcome her with open arms, bringing her into the family in a way that will be special. They'll do that for you, Nigel. You're the one who always had the time for them, would give up what you wanted to do to help them or go somewhere with them. Nolan and I didn't always do that, too busy living life." He watched the emotions on his brother's face. "Don't worry about Mom and Dad. They'll be shocked at how it happened, but not at who. Dad will want to march right into the town and take on the mayor, if I know him. Mom will be right at his side."

Nigel laughed at the image of his father marching into Sanctuary. "He'd win, that's for sure. The mayor wouldn't have a chance." He paused, a thought crossing his mind. "Where are Mom and Dad right now?"

"Right now? I'd say in a town near here. They knew we were heading here. The girls are there as well. They've made it into a family retreat if there are any questions asked as to why we're all here. Angus stayed with them, just in case we needed to call in reinforcements."

Havan spoke from where she stood, next to Nigel. "They have done that? No questions asked, just showed up?" She turned to study Nigel. "They would do that for you, Nigel?"

Nigel reached out an arm to draw her to his side, holding her tightly to him. "They would and have, love. And for you. Even though they don't know about you, they have reached out through these guys here to help. They know I've been staying with you and your father." He frowned, as his eyes searched and found Jackson. "Dad said something about a Jax and that he would do anything to help me."

Jackson had looked up at his words, a strange look crossing his face. "Who's your father, Nigel? I don't think we ever talked much about your family."

"Dad? He's Nixon Wells. Mom's name is Naomi."

"Nix? Well, well, well. It is a small world, then, isn't it? Your father and I were roommates in college, all four years. We lost track of one another not long after we graduated. I know your mother as well."

The three brothers stared at him, not quite sure if he was telling the truth, and then seeing the younger man in the older man from the photos their father had shared.

Nigel walked over to stand in front of Jackson. "You were a good friend to him, Jackson. He has talked about you over the years, sad that he lost contact with you." He paused, hands running through his hair. "Who would have thought?"

"God did, Nigel. He planned it all." Jackson turned to his daughter, catching her close to him. "You've heard me speak of Nixon?" When she nodded, he pointed at Nigel. "I was trying to think who this one reminded me of. He is so much like his father when we were in college."

"Nigel looks like Dad, but not as much as Nolan. He has a lot of Dad's mannerisms." Nevin grinned at the face Nigel made. "It's true, Nige. You are like Dad that way."

"I know. Now, to change the subject, how and when do we leave? We're not going to be able to walk out in daylight like we planned, not now. I can guarantee he'll have men watching us."

Chapter 8

Two hours after midnight, Jackson roused the men and then Havan, setting them to straightening away what they could, keeping the lights low. He knew the cabin was under surveillance and wanted to keep their activities as quiet as possible. Few words were spoken.

Nigel watched as Havan headed for her father's room, backpack in hand, beckoning him to follow. He frowned as he did so. There wasn't a back door there, so what was she up to?

"Here, in the corner here. Dad has his dresser attached to the floor. Tilt it that way, Nigel. There's a tunnel under the house. We found it by accident one year and Dad has dug it out further and strengthened it where it needs to be. It will bring us out on the deer trail. They'll never see us." She dropped her pack down and scurried down the ladder, a lit flashlight in her hand as she looked back up at him. "Come on. We need to get moving. Your brothers are behind you."

Nigel glanced behind him. Sure enough, the three men stood there. He could hear Jackson moving around in the other rooms. He dropped easily down beside her, moving away as the other men followed him. Havan grasped his hand.

"This way. Dad will lock the door. No one will find it. It's too hidden."

"I wondered why your Dad had a clear dresser top. Now I know. How far is it?"

"A couple of miles. Come on. Let's get moving. The further away we are by daylight, the better it will be. They won't know where we've gone."

"Unless they put up a drone." Nolan's droll voice sounded through the tunnel.

Havan laughed at that. "They won't see us. The canopy of the trees is too thick."

Havan finally stopped at the entrance of the tunnel, Nigel's arm around her as he stood for a moment, watching, listening. Nolan and Brett moved past him.

"Which way are we heading?" Nevin's voice was low.

"To the right, to the east. We'll be heading into the sunrise. About five miles past here, we can access the route Nigel picked out. It's a rough route, but doable. Mostly sheltered, which is what we want." Jackson stood beside Nigel, his eyes on the two younger men as they searched the area. Nevin flanked Havan.

"When we move out, I'll lead. Nevin behind me. Then you, Nigel. Havan next. Nolan and Brett behind her. We need to keep you two as sheltered as possible." Jackson shared a long look with Nevin, who nodded, agreeing with the plan.

Hours later, dusty, tired, and hungry, they paused at the edge of town. It had been a long trek, fraught with danger from falling rocks and loose shale but they had made it without anyone falling or being hurt.

Nigel handed Havan a water bottle before drinking from his own and then pointing with it.

"Nevin and Nolan's trucks are over there. We'll ride with Nevin. Your Dad and Brett with ride with Nolan."

"Just where are we heading now, Nigel?" Havan was tired and frustrated, not liking the feeling of having no control over what happened next, besides feeling dusty and dirty.

"We'll head to the house Mom and Dad have. We'll be safe there."

"And just how do you know that?" Havan refused to move, even though Nigel was trying his best to get her into the truck.

"I know because I know my parents and my family. They will have a house that has good security and a good line of sight around it. That's how we do things." He sighed. "Please, Havan. Just get in the truck. We'll show you what I mean, but I can't if you don't cooperate." Nigel was trying not to show his frustration as her rebellion, even though he could understand it.

She shot him a mutinous look before she saw her father shaking his head, an amused look on his face. She turned, reaching for a truck door, to find Nigel ahead of her, tucking her into the back seat and sliding in beside her.

"You can sit in the front, Nigel." She waited for his response, getting none. "Nigel? The front seat?"

Nevin began to laugh. "It's how we do it when we're providing protection, Havan. The parties sit in the back seat with their bodyguard."

Havan finally sat back, disgruntled before she sighed, her head resting down on Nigel's shoulder. "I'm sorry." Her words were barely audible. "I shouldn't have acted like that." Her hand was clasped tight in his at her words.

"It's okay, love. You've been through a lot, and right now, you're heading to meet people you're not sure you want to meet." Nigel and Nevin shared a look before Nevin nodded. That thought had never crossed his mind. "They'll love you, Havan. Just for who you are and because of your Dad."

She nodded, then yawned. "I'm sorry. I get grumpy when I'm tired."

"I never would have noticed." Nigel braced himself for the elbow that never came and tilted his head to watch her face.

"Nigel?" Nevin's voice was quiet from the front seat.

"Yeah, Nevin?"

"Have you thought any more about a motive for the marriage?"

Nigel nodded. "I have. I've asked Brett to run a computer search when we reach the house. And Angus. I want to search the financials on the mayor."

"You're suspecting something?"

"I am, and until I'm sure, I don't want to say anything." His eyes dropped back to Havan, who was almost asleep. "How far to the house?"

"Five minutes. Do you think your lady will stay awake?"

Nigel shrugged, even as a smile crossed his face. "I have no idea. I don't like the thoughts of having her sleep and then waking her again."

"If she's sleeping, I'll go in and clear away everyone with some excuse. Your room is at the top of the stairs, first door on the left."

"Thanks, Nevin." Nigel watched the stores, surprising Nevin with a request to stop.

"Sure. Will you be long?"

"No, not long." Nigel was gone from the truck and into a store that Nevin couldn't see, not quite sure what his brother was up to.

Nigel turned to head for the truck, tucking his purchase into his pocket when he stopped, his eyes on another store. He shot a look back at the truck and then headed into the store, asking for help. He was soon back in the truck, shaking his head at Nevin's questioning look.

"Not for you, Nevin."

"Are you sure?" Nevin grinned at his brother.

Nigel just shook his head again and watched the traffic as Nevin drove away, his hand finding Havan's again. Stepping from the truck a few minutes later, he studied the large house and nodded. Just what he would have chosen. He stooped to watch Havan, knowing he didn't have the heart to awaken her. He simply scooped her into his arms and grabbed the bag he had left on the seat before Nevin could.

Havan roused a couple of hours later, a hand rubbing at her eyes. She sat up, fear coursing through her for a moment, not quite sure where she was before she felt the bed sink down and her eyes found Nigel.

"Hi." Nigel watched as she yawned again, before reaching to wrap her into his arms. "Did you have a nice nap?"

"I think so. What time is it?"

"Just after 4. Listen. We need to talk. First, about Sanctuary." He watched her face, seeing a shuttered look come across it. "I found out why the mayor was so intent on marrying off his daughters."

"And that would be?" She leaned back so she could watch him.

"He would inherit millions with each daughter's marriage, but they had to be married by a certain date, one year apart. Today was the deadline for the oldest one."

"So that's why he was so insistent that we come back to town? He wanted to declare the marriage illegal and then marry you off to her?"

Nigel nodded. "I would think so. He doesn't get it. I would never have agreed even if our marriage wasn't registered." He paused, his hands finding hers, his thumb rubbing at her ring. "I regret the way this happened." He felt her tense and draw back, trying to free her hands. "I repeat. I regret the way it happened. I don't regret that it was you. I think you've been the one I was waiting for." He looked up, his heart in his eyes. "I have fallen in love with you, Havan. I would like to be the one to grow old with you. If you will have me."

She stared at him, her mouth open before she remembered to snap it closed. He sighed as she didn't respond, and made to rise, before her hands tightened on his. Tears, the first he had seen from her, sparkled in her eyes as she nodded.

"I love you too, Nigel. I thought it was one sided and wouldn't have said anything for the world." Her voice was barely above a whisper.

"You do?" He wrapped her in a hug, arms tight, before he set her back and reached into a pocket. "I would like to do something about these bands. But first, will you wear this for me?" He held up a beautiful sapphire ring and watched as her eyes widened. Slipping it on her finger, he reached to gently kiss her.

"About the mayor." She asked moments later, her mind going back to her home town. "Did he really think he'd get away with that?"

"Apparently he did. Brett did some research for me and found that out. He also found out the mayor is highly in debt to some not so nice people."

"But, Nigel. Wait." She looked at him, fear on her face. "What happens now? We've run. He'll track us down. Who goes after us? Him or the other men?"

"That's what our guys are working on. It will take some time but they'll figure it out." Nigel rose and paced. "We just have to stay out of sight until they figure it out."

"And staying out of sight, how? Not in a place like this. They'll know it was your family that rented it." She watched him smile. "No. Tell me they didn't."

He nodded. "Dad bought it about a month ago. This was where I was supposed to be heading when I took a wrong turn, that turned into the right one." He sat down again, reaching for her hand. "I need to talk to them, tell them about us. We have this big formal family dinner tonight." He watched as she paled and tried to pull away from him again. "It's okay. If you refuse to go, so do I. You're my main concern. They will understand."

"Nigel. They're your family. You can't refuse to go." She was horrified at the thought. "Dad and I can hang out here together."

He began to laugh. "Sorry. Your Dad and my Dad have renewed their friendship. He's planning on being there tonight."

She finally tugged her hand away from him and rose, beginning to pace. "Nigel. I can't go. I have nothing but jeans. And for a formal dinner, that won't do."

"Havan, love, if that's all you have to wear, then so will I. But, I did a little shopping while you were asleep, before we reached here." He rose and headed for the closet, pulling her with him, to stand her in front of the dark blue formal dress he had found. "I bought this just for you. I hope it fits."

She stood, mouth open, as she stared at it, then at him. "It's beautiful. And shoes too." She reached out a hand to touch the dress, the other hand covering her mouth. "You shouldn't have, Nigel. It could have been money wasted."

"Never, love. Never that. If you had only looked at it and loved it, never worn it, it would have been fine. Now, we have about thirty minutes to dress. Can we do that? I'll be right across the hall from you."

Thirty minutes later, Nigel stood, watching Havan as she paced. She's beautiful, Lord, and she's mine. Thank you. Now, help me to keep her safe. I know we're not done with that man. He walked towards her, stopping her in her tracks, and pulled a necklace from his pocket.

"Nigel?" Havan was laughing, almost in tears again. "What did you do? Buy out the stores?"

He grinned as he fastened the necklace and fingered the locket. "We'll need to have photos done for this." He stooped to kiss her once more just as a knock came to the door. He sighed. "Talk about bad timing. It's likely my parents."

She backed away from him, her eyes huge. "I'm not ready for this, Nigel."

He drew her forward again as he called out for his parents to enter. Naomi and Nixon Wells entered, their eyes on their son, before they reached out to hug him. Havan had slipped behind him, not quite ready to face his parents.

"Nigel? You're well now?" His mother was concerned.

"I am, Mom. I have very good care while I was sick." He paused, searching for words, the hesitation so unlike him his parents exchanged a glance before his mother noticed movement behind him and stepped to the side.

"And who do we have here, Nigel?" She studied the younger woman, seeing apprehension on her face, before her eyes caught the blue of Havan's eyes. "It's Jackson's daughter. I would recognize those eyes anywhere. Welcome. Jackson didn't say you were with him." She reached to draw Havan into a hug, a hug Havan responded to, feeling a mother's arms around her for the first time she could remember.

Nixon hugged her as well before turning a look on his son Nigel knew only too well. They needed to talk and talk now.

"Mom? Dad? We have some time before dinner. Can we sit? I need to explain some things to you." He reached for Havan's hand, not seeing the speculative look his father shot him, before he seated her on the couch, sitting next to her, his hand tight on hers.

"Nigel?" His mother's voice broke into his thoughts. "What is it you need to talk to us about?"

"About what happened." He explained about the law and how Sanctuary was. He caught a sound from his father and looked up, seeing the understanding there, knowing his father was on his side, no matter what he said.

His eyes on Havan's face as she watched him, he didn't see the looks his parents were exchanging, a puzzled frown on his mother's. "About that law." He sighed. "I sound like I'm repeating myself. I was really sick, as you know, when I reached Sanctuary. Havan stepped in, and we were married. Mom, Dad, meet Havan O'Leary Wells."

Havan stared at him, wondering if he could have softened the blow, not willing to look at the older couple. She jumped as she felt an arm come around her and turned to face Naomi, finding tears in the mother's eyes.

"Havan? Oh, how wonderful! Thank you! If you didn't already have Nigel's heart, you would still be part of our family." She hugged the younger woman, startling her. Hugs had not been plentiful when she got older, her father being more reserved.

Nixon stood, imposing in his height, before he too hugged Havan and then kissed her cheek. A hand on his son's shoulder shook slightly, and Nigel nodded at the emotions his father was hiding. They would talk more later.

Nigel finally watched as his parents walked away, knowing the younger couple needed some time. He reached to encircle Havan with his arms, drawing her back to him.

"Not quite what you expected?"

She shook her head. "No. Your parents are lovely. I didn't expect that kind of welcome."

"You're Jackson's daughter. That made you welcome. But most important, you're my wife. That makes you more welcome than that. It's the way they are." He sighed, knowing she still had the gauntlet to run of his sisters. He finally rose, a hand out for her to grip. He simply smiled at the tightness of her hand on his as they walked down the stairs.

He gave a quiet laugh at her comment that she would rather face the mayor than any more of his family.

"They don't bite. Well, maybe a bit. Nora and Noelle will just have to learn to share."

She stopped at the entrance to the dining room, her eyes uplifted to him, before she smiled. "I can do that. At least, I think I can. It might be tough." She sighed, her eyes searching his. "Nigel, we really do need to talk about the future and what our plans are."

Nigel smiled down at her, his eyes taking in her beauty. "We will, love. We will. We don't have to make any plans tonight. Tonight, I just want to show off my beautiful bride. No matter how we married, you are the love of my life. Never forget that. No matter what we face, and I know we're not done with the mayor as yet, I will be there to defend you."

"Thank you."

They were in a world of their own, not hearing the conversation cease or the perplexed looks on the faces of the four younger woman. Nigel had simply asked the men not to say anything, that it was his right and duty to introduce Havan to the family. They had agreed, knowing they would face questions later that night.

Nora and Noelle approached them, Nevin's wife, Beth, and Nolan's wife, Amy, behind them.

"Nigel?" Nora's quiet question raised his head.

"Nora." He swept her into a hug, then moved to do the same to Noelle, holding his favourite sister just a little bit longer, before moving on to hug his brothers' wives. He turned, his arm drawing Havan to him.

"Havan, these are my sisters. Nora, Brett's wife. Noelle, Angus' wife. And then we have Nevin's wife, Beth, and Nolan's wife, Amy. Ladies, please welcome to the family my wife, Havan."

The ladies were quiet for a moment, studying Nigel before they turned to Havan, suddenly swarming her and making her feel welcome. Nigel finally pulled her free to head for the table, seating her beside her father and then finding his own seat.

/ *Chapter 9*

Nigel looked up the next morning, setting his tea mug back down, as he heard footsteps approaching and the rustle of paper. He never thought he'd like tea as much as he did, but Havan and Jackson had won him over to it.

"Nigel. We have a huge problem." Nolan slid into a chair across from him.

"And that would be?"

"The mayor. He's in town, looking for you two. It won't be long before he finds this place." Nolan shifted the papers he had laid on the table, trying to find the words he needed.

"I figured that he would. What now?"

Nolan shrugged, his eyes on his brother. "It's your call. We can keep you two here, send you back home, or send you back to the cabin."

"Back to the cabin?" Nigel sat back, not having thought of that. "Why there?"

"Because they wouldn't think to look there for you right away."

"But there is still the problem of us getting back there. We can't just walk back. I won't do that to Havan."

Nolan nodded. "That's what I said you'd say."

Nigel began to laugh. "Did you even make sense?"

Nolan looked up, realized what he had said, and began to laugh. "No, I don't think I did. I've been awake for too many hours."

"Too many hours on this already, brother. Let's get it figured out before we head home at the end of the week." He sighed. "At least for you guys. I'm not sure where I'll be."

"Talk to Havan, and I mean really talk. It's both your futures and you need to be in agreement on this." Nolan looked down. "I'm afraid for you, Nigel. This man is scary. We've been digging into his past. There are rumours that he's killed people to get where he is."

"And that would be a fact." The men looked up at Havan's voice before Nigel rose and drew her to a chair beside him, seating her and then pouring her a cup of tea. "He killed my mother. Not with his own hands, but he prevented her from having medical assistance. That's the kind of man you're dealing with."

Nolan stared at her. "He did that? How old were you?" At her comment of two months, he stared even harder, before he looked down. "He must not have been mayor for long then."

"About a year or less. He just came into town and took over. I have no idea what happened to the old mayor or council. Dad would know. I have never heard them mentioned." She looked up at Nolan, a shadow on her face. "I've often wondered if he had them killed. I hear about their wives leaving town with their families, but not the men."

Nigel reached for her hand, grasping it lightly. "We'll figure it out, love."

They talked for a while longer, trying to come up with a plan, before Havan became frustrated and rose. She wanted this over. She wanted to go home, only she didn't know where home was any more. She paused at the kitchen doorway, to turn and watch Nigel as he talked to his brother. They were so alike, she thought, but so different.

Stopping at the living room door as she heard his sisters talking, she hesitated about entering. She didn't see her father standing behind her, his eyes assessing her, worrying about her.

Havan drew in a deep breath as she heard Nora's words. They cut deep, implying that she had trapped Nigel into marriage, that they would have to investigate further. Nora's voice was almost strident, although low. Havan turned, tears streaming down her face, running for the stairs and her room, where she ran to the window and stood, a hand raised to the pane as the tears continued to flow.

Nolan had been approaching her, to ask her a question, when he saw her turn and run and watched as Jackson turned as well before turning back and heading for the living room, where he too stopped at the doorway. Nolan approached quietly, hearing Nora's words, and Noelle's attempts to make her be quiet.

Nolan brushed past Jackson and stalked over to Nora, standing in front of her, anger flowing from him.

Noelle gave a gasp as she saw him. She didn't think she had ever seen him that angry. He was one who was slow to anger but when he did become mad, it took a long while for him to cool off.

"Nora!" Nolan's voice was low and cutting.

Nora looked up, unrepentant. As the youngest in the family she had always been allowed a bit of leniency but never to this extent. She stared at her brother, a frown on her face.

"What do you want, Nolan? Noelle and I are having a conversation."

"A conversation that is mostly gossip and hurt." Nolan held up a hand, shaking his head at Nora, who finally saw through the anger on his face and saw the hurt in his eyes and wondered what had caused it. "Havan heard you, Nora. She heard every word you said about trapping Nigel into the marriage." He paused, trying to bite back his anger. "You are so wrong. And I am so angry at you. Nigel will hear about this, and I can guarantee you, he will take Havan and leave. I don't know if he'll ever come back, thanks to you. You deserve that if he doesn't. The rest of us don't. You've gone too far this time." He turned at that and stalked away, heading for Nigel to send him to find his wife.

Jackson walked forward, his eyes full on sorrow as he watched the young woman.

Noelle stood and hugged him. He thanked her before he turned to Nora.

"You will never know the hurt you have just inflicted on my daughter. I thought better of my friend's family. Obviously, I was wrong. Havan has never known the friendship of young women. Not in our town. We're the outsiders, not allowed to mingle with the towns people no matter how much we want to. That's the kind of control that's there. She has never known a woman's touch, not until last night when she met your mother and fell in love with her. Her mother died when she was two months old." He paused, sorrow coursing through him. "She is in a situation now where she needs that and won't have it, because Nigel will leave with her. I have no idea where they'll go. You have just torn the family apart, Nora, by your own words."

He turned to Noelle. "Please thank your parents for me. I'll be leaving as soon as I pack, and that will be in about two minutes." He shook his head as he turned and walked away.

Noelle stood, staring at her sister. "You've gone and done it well this time, Nora. Thanks a lot." She turned, tears burning in her own eyes, running to find Angus, knowing he would comfort her, but that would never heal the breach in the family.

Brett stood in the French doors, listening to the conversation and sighed. He loved Nora dearly, but had warned her the night before to be very careful with her words and to watch what she said around Havan. He knew Havan was that fragile at this time and needed all the support she could be given.

"Nora? Care to explain?"

Brett's voice behind her had her spinning. "What? You too? Don't you find it suspicious too?"

"Actually, no, I don't. Not with the research I've done on that mayor and town. He's all they've said and more. Do you know he prevented Jackson from getting medical help for his wife, that's why she died? She didn't need to."

Nora stared at him, finally understanding what was being said. "Brett.. I didn't know. What did I do?"

"You've about destroyed a young woman, who is deeply loved by a brother who has done just about anything for you. You've destroyed that relationship, Nora. He will never be the same with you again. And right now, I can't begin to tell you how disappointed and hurt I am." He held up a hand. "No, don't come near me. Go, find your Bible, and spend time with God. You've been neglecting that, and it's showing. What happened to you, Nora? You're so different from the woman I married, some days I don't know you at all."

Nora watched as he walked away, knowing he was right. She turned to the doorway, hesitating as she looked at the stairs, before she trudged up them, stopping at her brother's door, hearing low voices coming from it, one with tears in it, and realized how she had hurt them. She should have talked to Havan, she now knew. She headed on past to her room, her eyes filled with tears. She had hurt her favourite brother and knew he might never forgive her.

Nigel had looked up from the paperwork when Nolan came back, a distressed look on his face. He stood, dropping the papers on the table, knowing something was really wrong.

"Nolan? What did she say?"

Nolan just shook his head. "Nora upset her. She overhead a conversation that should never have happened." He looked behind him. "I think you need to go to her." He laid a hand on his brother's arm as he brushed past him. "I spoke with Nora. Jackson was there. Brett heard as well."

Nigel sighed, his eyes raised to the ceiling. "She really went and did that, did she? I think Havan and I will be leaving this afternoon, Nolan. She doesn't need this. I'm sorry." His eyes showed how deeply disturbed he was, regret on his face.

"Believe me, Nigel. I understand. It's best that you do. Jackson's neighbour has a cabin you two can use. They won't find you there. Charlie will take you out there. He's been visiting Josh on and off for the last few days, just in case we needed someone out there. I suspect Jackson will leave as well."

Chapter 10

Closing the bedroom door quietly behind him, Nigel leaned against it for a moment, his eyes on his young bride, sorrow, hurt and anger mixed in his heart. First, he had to ensure his wife was okay. Then, they would leave. He hated having to do that but Havan came first.

His arms coming around her startled Havan before she turned, her own arms clinging to him as she sobbed, heartbroken at the hurtful words she had overheard. She knew she had not trapped him. Everyone else seemed to understand.

Nigel's own tears flowed, his heart also breaking. This was not how he had pictured their day, not at all. He just tightened his arms around her and then scooped her into his arms, finding the arm chair and settling down with her on his knee, cradling her tight to him.

She finally tilted her head back to look up at him. "Nigel?"

"Nolan told me Nora said some things. Not what she actually said, but I can guess. I think we need to leave, Havan. We need to work out what we want and we can't here." He sighed. "Nora was out of line, a way out of line. Brett has dealt with her. I think your Dad had words for her as well."

"But she's your sister. You can't just walk away from her."

"Trust me, love. I will. If I don't, she'll be told off thoroughly and that has already been done. She's Brett's wife. He has to deal with her. Nolan overhead what Nora was saying and said Brett did too."

"This is so wrong, Nigel. I shouldn't be coming between you and your family. Everyone will always think that I trapped you."

"Never, my love. Never that. We know better. So does your father and my family. Nora's been different lately, and we can't figure out why." He sighed, his arms tightening around her. "Where would you like to go?"

She shrugged. "I have no idea. We can't go back to the cabin, that's a given."

"Nolan said something about an extra cabin at Josh's?"

She shook her head. "They'll be watching that. I know them well enough to know they'll have men in the woods watching all the outsiders, waiting for one of them to help us." She laid her head back on his shoulder, feeling the strength in him, not just the physical strength but his emotional and spiritual strength and thanked God he was her husband. With him beside her, she could face life, she thought.

"Okay. Then, we'll need to come up with a plan." He watched her face, seeing something there that caused him to frown. "What are you thinking?"

"We could always head right into Sanctuary and confront him."

"We're not at that point yet, love. Soon. The guys are still gathering evidence and talking to law enforcement. Apparently Mayor Brown is on the radar of more than one department."

"That's good." She yawned. "I'm sorry. All of a sudden, I'm just so tired."

"Emotions do that. I have seen Noelle drop off when she's been really stressed." His arms tightened even more. "Just relax and sleep, my love. You've been going without enough sleep ever since I didn't know I met you. I'm not going anywhere."

His head on hers as she slept, Nigel thought through everything and her request that they go to Sanctuary. He knew that would be coming but he wasn't ready yet to let her go that route. Soon, he thought. His heart turned to prayer, asking God to help him forgive his sister, and to bring the situation to a quick end.

He finally stood, walking over to gently lay her on the bed and reaching for a blanket to cover her. He stooped, a kiss dropping on her hair, before he stood, eyes staring ahead, determination in his manner. He turned, heading for his father. There was one place they could go, that no one would find them. He just had to make sure no one else was there.

Nixon watched Nigel's face as he paced the study, having heard what had happened earlier. He knew Brett would deal with Nora, but he would have a talk with her as well. He sighed. This is so wrong, Lord. This should not be happening.

"The cottage is free, Nigel, if that's what you're trying to ask. I had it checked out earlier in the week. Charlie will take you and Havan there."

"Thanks, Dad." Nigel stood at a window, hands jammed into his pockets.

"Havan's sleeping right now. I think I'll just pack her up and leave now, before Mom gets back. I don't want to be here when she goes after Nora."

Nixon gave a small laugh. "Go pack, Nigel. I'll keep everyone away. We'll keep in touch." He watched with sadness as his son walked away, knowing his family had shattered and for once he had no idea how to put it back together, just knowing it would never be the same. Determination grew in his heart to deal with the mayor of Sanctuary quickly and get his family back together.

Nigel quietly moved around the bedroom, his eyes darting to Havan as he packed their things, including their formal wear. He had loved her in the dress the night before. She had been so beautiful, he thought, as he stooped to grab her shoes. He sighed. This is not right, Lord. I shouldn't be having to leave, to go on the run with my bride.

He handed Nolan the packs, not looking at him, knowing his brother wanted to say something but wouldn't. He turned to Havan, sighing to himself once more, before he gathered her to him and walked away from the room and away from the house, settling her into Charlie's SUV, not looking back, not seeing the family standing watching them leave.

Charlie shot a look at the younger man. He had worked for Nixon for years and was close to Nixon's age. He looked on the family as his children and would do just about anything for them.

Havan finally roused, her eyes blinking open before she sat up abruptly, fear in her face. Nigel was there in a moment, sitting on the bed beside her.

"Where are we?"

"At our cottage. No one knows we're here." He watched as her face relaxed. "It's just us. Charlie brought us and then headed back. We have everything we need for now. Dad will be in touch."

"It's still not right, Nigel." She shoved away the blanket and stumbled to her feet, searching for her pack. "I need a shower. Where are my things?" She knew she was changing the subject but the other one was just too hard at the moment.

"In the closet. The bathroom is the door in front of you."

He stood for a moment, watching her search for her things and then shut the door. He headed for the kitchen, knowing they needed to eat but that neither one of them likely felt much like it.

Havan hesitated at the table beside sliding into a chair, her eyes on the sandwich Nigel set in front of her before sitting beside her. She eyed him, catching him watching her. "You could sit on the other side of the table, you know. There's lots of room."

He grinned, knowing she was just rephrasing her comment from the day before. "Nope. I like this side. The company's the best." He ducked the playful swat she aimed at him before he reached for her hand, bowing his head in prayer.

She finally sat back, shoving her plate away. "Thank you, Nigel. I needed to eat. I didn't think I could though."

"I didn't think I could either." He watched her closely, seeing the sorrow still lingering in her eyes. "For the next few days, it's just us. Dad said he'd be around in about three days."

She nodded, her finger moving a crumb around on the tabletop. "What about your family, Nigel? We can't just walk away from them."

"We haven't. We're giving each other space, space that is badly needed between myself and a certain sister." He held up his hand as she went to protest. "We've had words before, but she has never hurt anyone with her words the way she did you. She has to learn that you come first with me, just like she does with Brett."

Havan nodded. "I get that, but she's still your sister. You can't just walk away from her, not for long. You need to talk it out."

"We will at some point, but right now, this is our time. We need to talk, figure out things. One of which is where we live."

"About that. Where will we live, Nigel? I have no idea where your home is, what it's like, if you can live anywhere else."

He nodded. "A lot to cover. Right now, I'm on a leave of absence. I need to figure out what I really want to do."

"I thought you worked for your family." Havan studied him, seeing something that gave her hope she wouldn't have to leave her home.

"I do, but I'm not really needed there. Anyone can do what I do." He grinned suddenly. "Maybe I should move to Sanctuary and run for mayor."

She finally remembered to shut her mouth before she shook her head, a smile crossing her face. "Now, that I can see you doing. We'll work it out. When do you have to report back to the office?"

"In about three weeks, give or take." He rose, gathering the remnants of their meal and heading for the sink, Havan following after him to fill the sink with water and then wash their dishes. Her eyes raised to the outdoors, she watched the lake, before she dried her hands and moved outside to stand on the deck. She finally moved down to the dock, pulling off her socks and shoes, rolling up her jeans legs and sitting, her feet just reaching the water. Nigel dropped down beside her, an arm around her.

"This is so peaceful, Nigel. I could live here very easily." Her head on his shoulder, she didn't see the startled look on his face.

"It is nice. Dad bought this as an investment. He would let me have it, I know, very easily. We could live here. It's winterized and easy to maintain."

She looked up at him, to find him watching her. "You'd do that? Live here?"

He nodded. "Right now, this is what I need. With you." He watched as she blushed, knowing they still needed to talk through a lot of things. "That sunset. It's always beautiful here, even in winter."

She nodded, her eyes roaming the area. "How safe are we really, Nigel?"

"Here? About as safe as anywhere. This isn't in Dad's name. It's in Mom's name, so it takes so looking to find it. That's not to say someone won't find us. I pray they don't."

They sat in silence, listening to the nights sounds, the lapping of the waves against the dock and the shore before Havan spoke.

"I would like to live here, if I can't live in Sanctuary. It's peaceful. I need that. My life has been so sheltered though, Nigel, I have no idea what I do or don't want."

"One day at a time, love. That's all we can do. One day at a time." He hugged her tighter to him. "We can go back to my place for a while and see how you make out. I want you to be happy. If you can't be happy in the country outside of my town, I move. It's that simple."

She nodded, knowing he meant just that. "Where God leads, Nigel. That's how I was raised. We wait for him." She sat for a moment. "Please, don't let Nora's words destroy your relationship with her. She didn't know. I can forgive her, even though the words hurt."

"Unfortunately, she has already been spoken to. Your father heard. He was nice by what Nolan said, and gentle with her. She needs to apologize to you. Accept it when she does. She can be a bit of a hothead. Mom and Dad have worked on her for years about that, and now Brett has to deal with it."

"I get that, Nigel, but this was such a shock. I might have said something similar had the roles been reversed."

He tilted his head to watch her face in the dimming light. "I don't think so. You don't have it in you to hurt like that."

"I could, you know. I feel that way towards the Mayor."

"He's given you reason to." He stood, reaching to help her to her feet, bending to gather their shoes and socks before wrapping an arm around her. "Head for bed, love. The room you woke up is yours. I'll be down the hall." He shook his head as she looked at him. "We need to talk first. We have decisions to make. Let's do that over the next few days."

She searched his face as they stopped in the kitchen, finally reaching to pull his head down and kissing him. "Thank you, Nigel." Her words were barely audible as she walked away. Nigel watched her go, sighing to himself. Lord, this is not what I thought life would be like. You'll have to lead.

He stood for a moment before setting their shoes near the door and then wandering through the cottage, securing it for the night. He stood for a moment, staring down into the empty fire grate, a resolve firming in his heart. He would face the mayor shortly and win, he decided. Havan and her father, and yes, everyone in Sanctuary and the outsiders, all deserved that resolution.

Havan tossed and turned that night, not finding the sleep she needed. She finally rose about 4 a.m., quietly moving through the cottage, reaching to make herself a cup of tea before curling up in a chair in the living room, her eyes on the floor, her thoughts chaotic. She was never like this. She always thought clearly. Being around Nigel changed that on her. She was so worried he would be hurt because of her. She sighed. No, because of himself too. The mayor was desperate to find them, she knew. How long would they be hidden and safe?

She finally slept, not hearing Nigel as he rose hours later, stopping to search her room for her, finally finding her curled up asleep in the chair. He smiled before touching her curls. He loved the softness of them. He moved through to the kitchen, making tea for himself and setting her china cup ready for hers. He walked through to the deck, standing so he could see the door but also see the lake, a hand gripping the railing. Something was about to break loose, he knew, and he had no idea of what or when. It was just coming.

He turned as he heard soft footsteps. Havan stood beside him, her eyes on the lake, before she moved closer to him, her arm wrapping around his and her hand finding his.

"Our rings. Nigel, you said you wanted to do something about them. Just what?"

He smiled, knowing she was avoiding asking the questions they needed to ask. "I would like to marry you again, Havan. This time, you get to dress up in a white gown, veil if you want, flowers, attendants, your Dad walking you to me. Me up in front in a suit and tie, awake and aware of what's happening. New rings that we have picked out ourselves."

"Oh, I would love to do that. It sounds lovely." She sighed, her head against his arm. "But when? We're in hiding. Your family and Dad are far away, aren't they?" She looked up at his silence. "They are, aren't they?"

"Far enough not to intrude but near enough if we need them. The cottage is close to Sanctuary." He pointed across the lake. "If we were to row across there, a five mile walk would have us there."

"We're that close to home? No wonder I like it here. I am home. I've wandered the woods on that side of the lake for years."

"That's what I thought. That's why I wanted to come here with you."

"Have you heard from your brothers yet?"

He shook his head. "Nope. I haven't looked. I don't intend to for a few days. I need the break from everything. That was my plan when I set out from home. I wasn't going to look at emails, the internet, the phone, not unless I needed to. It's still my plan."

"Don't, Nigel. You need to keep in touch with them. Set aside an hour a day to deal with what you need to. I can find something to do in that time." She looked back at the house. "Someone has set up a great library. I could get lost in there. I have books, but nothing like this. I've always wanted a room called a library."

"Have you? Then I'm glad Mom did that. She loves to read, has a book near her at all the time." He stopped, his mind racing. "This may sound strange, love, but does your town have a library?"

She shook her head. "No. Why?"

"Then people don't have access to outside communication?"

"Some do, but for the most part, the mayor has banned all electronic devices and the internet. We need to get him out of there." She moved her head so she could look up at him. "Still thinking of running for mayor? Elections are coming up, you know. If you registered now, you could run."

"That's something to think about. I just might. Think I'd get voted in?"

She shrugged. "Depends on how strongly he would move to prevent that and how tired the people are of his control."

"I would think they would be really tired by now. Dad mentioned something in passing about hearing from someone there who wanted to talk to him. He never heard from that man again.”

“Oh no. If the mayor found out, that man could be dead.”

“That’s what we’re afraid of. Or else put somewhere he can’t talk to Dad.”

“That too. He would do just that.”

Nigel sighed as he felt his phone vibrate. “Force of habit to stick this in my pocket. I meant to leave it on the counter.” He frowned as he looked down at it.

“Nigel?” When he didn’t respond, she touched his hand, bringing his attention to her. “Nigel? What is it?”

“Dad says the mayor found the house and tried to get in. They’ve kept him out and sent him away, but they’re sure he left men to watch. That means they can’t head our way any time soon.”

“He really did?” At his nod, she broke free and began to pace, finally stopping in front of him. “You have an advantage your family no longer has. You have me. I know the mayor. I know who his friends and enemies are.” She reached for his hand. “Come on, love. Let’s go do some work. Until this is behind us, our lives can’t go on.”

Nigel followed, his heart quickening at the endearment she had uttered. It was the first time she had done that. He found his laptop, set it up, and placed her in front of it. "This is a word processing program. Are you familiar with one?"

She shook her head. "Not really. I just type?"

"You do." He grinned at her. "This is modern technology for you." He watched as she tentatively touched the keyboard, her eyes huge as she saw the letters on the screen.

"Oh, I like this. You'll never get this back, you know."

He began to laugh. "It's okay if I don't. Now, let's see what we can do. Once you've remembered everything you can, I'll shoot it off to one of the guys and they'll follow up with the investigation."

She turned, her eyes still huge. "They can do that? Without us being there?"

"They can, my love. We just send it to them. We have encrypted emails that we use. No one can see them."

She nodded, her attention back on the laptop. She was thrilled, she thought. She had heard of these for years, but never seen one, let alone used one. She just might not give it back to Nigel when she was done.

Nigel shook his head as he walked away, pulling out his phone and checking his messages. He paused as he saw the urgent call from his Dad, knowing he would call him back in a moment, but needing some time in prayer. Things were heating up, he knew, and he wanted the peace that time would bring.

Havan hesitated at the bedroom door that Nigel was using, finding him with his head bowed as he sat on the bed. She approached quietly, slipping to a seating position beside him, his hand reaching for hers. When he looked up, his smile was bright and peaceful.

"Did you want something, love?" He reached to kiss her, finding her reaching for him in response.

"I did, but I think I like this better." She flushed red, embarrassed at her words and groaned. "Did I really just say that?"

He laughed, hugging her to him. "You did and you can't take those words back. I like this better too, but you have something you need to talk to me about."

She nodded, her hair brushing against his cheek. "I do." She tilted her head back. "You've never shaved your beard, not yet. Somehow I don't think that's how you usually look."

He grinned. "No, it wasn't. But a certain wife has said she likes it."

"And I wonder who that would be." She accepted his kiss, and then rose, pulling him with her. "I can tell you're at peace. Now, let me disturb that. I have the names you wanted, and I see a pattern, I think."

She sat him down in front of the laptop and began to rapidly talk, explaining who was who and how they were related or not to the mayor.

Nigel sat, staring at the screen, his mind racing. Some of the names he recognized, and a chill spread through him. He had been right. Mayor Brown was not acting alone, or else he was in so deep to the moneylenders, they had brought in people to watch him. He saved the list and sent it on to Angus, asking him to research the names. Angus was the researcher of the group, and Nigel knew he would leave no stone unturned to find out the answers they needed.

"I think we're on to something here, love. I recognize some of the names.

They're nasty people, to say the least. I just pray we don't get mixed up any further than we are."

He felt his phone vibrating and pulled it from his pocket, frowning as he recognized his father's number.

"Dad? You called earlier and I didn't get a chance to call you back. I see. That much, is it? Okay. Well, yeah, I guess." His eyes rested on Havan as she watched him, a frown on her face. "Okay. We'll be here. No, I don't think we'll be leaving any time soon. We have no vehicle, other than the row boat, and I'm not keen on pulling that out. Canoes? No, I didn't see them but I'm sure they're still here. I'll check later." He listened again, his finger rubbing along the table edge before Havan's hand closed over it, stilling his movements. "Right. Let me know when you have everything in place. Havan tells me we're right across from their place, almost. She knows the woods over there well. That right? Okay, then. Call me later."

He set his phone down, knowing he would have to purchase one for Havan and as soon as he could. He reached for Havan's hands, disturbed at what his father had reported

"Havan? I have some bad news."

"Dad?"

He nodded. "The mayor's men were waiting for him. He fought them off but ended up roughed up. He managed to get to Josh who drove him back to Dad's. It's not safe for him to go home. They are on the hunt for us."

"Oh, no. He's okay, though?" At his nod, she gripped his hands tighter. "We need to make plans, Nigel. It's only a matter of time before he figures out where we are. I can guarantee you he watches every one of the outsiders and knows exactly where they are and who they're with." She tried to rise, but his arm around her kept her still. "There's more?"

"There is. They've been able to track his financials. It's what we thought. He's highly in debt, has been for years, and was planning on the millions he was to inherit to bail himself out. He's reported to be very enraged at you for thwarting his plans. He's put a hit out on you."

"A hit? What do you mean?" She was puzzled, not aware of quite what he meant.

"It means he's hired someone to go after you and kill you.   I can't let that happen."

She froze, her eyes on him, shock in her face. "Nigel? To kill me? What happens if someone gets between me and that person?"

He shrugged.   "Depends on the contract. The hit man might take them out, or wait until he has a clear shot at you. And we have no idea who yet. The hit could come in any number of ways. We have to keep you safe. That may mean moving again." Once more, his arm held her to him. "I won't let them get you. Not if I can help it. But for now, we're safe. We can move around inside the cottage as we want. The windows are such that you can't see through them. We'll save our movements outdoors for after dark."

She nodded. "Can I call Dad and talk to him? Would that be okay?"

He nodded. "Tonight, I think. Dad said your father was sleeping right now. The doctor saw him and gave him a sedative. He was worried enough about you he was refusing to rest."

She rubbed her hands up and down her arms, her eyes on the tasteful decorations on the mantle. She rose, a frown on her face, walking over to pick up a vase.

"Nigel, this was not here this morning. Who put it here?"

He froze, then was at her side, taking the vase from her and searching it, a grim look on his face. "Havan. We need to leave and now. Quick. Pack some clothes and I'll grab some food." He reached for his phone, sending off a quick text to his face, then ran for his own backpack, and then the kitchen. Havan was with him in just a matter of minutes as he hesitated at the back door.

"Which way, Nigel?"

"I'm not sure. You know the area, don't you?"

"Somewhat. Why?"

"Where can we go to wait for help?"

"I know the place." She held up a hand, shaking her head. "Didn't your father say something about canoes? We could use those."

He watched her face for a moment, then nodded. He was aware of what she was up to. "He did. Let's head for there. Tonight's a nice night to be out, don't you think?"

He led the way to the boathouse, opening the door and finding the canoe, lifting it out to the water, sticking in their packs, and then helping her in, handing her one of the paddles before shoving them off from the shore.

"Where to, Havan?" His voice was barely audible.

"Let me think." She studied the shoreline, then dipped her paddle into the water, sending them off across the lake, before veering off to the right.

Nigel watched her concentration, knowing she would lead them to a place they could stay for now.

She finally steered them to the shore, waiting until he pulled the canoe up and then helped her out. She pointed to the canoe and then some bushes, helping him hide it, and then shouldering her back, gripped his hand and tugged him with her.

He followed, not quite sure where she was heading but trusting her to know where she was. He almost ran into her when she stopped.

"In here, Nigel. It's a cave that I discovered as a young girl. No one else knows about it. At least, I don't think so. It's pretty isolated. Isolated enough that the animals never used it. The deer trail leads right by it."

"Okay. Let me go first. Do you have a flashlight?"

She handed him one, and he entered the cave, shining the light cautiously around. "It looks okay. Nothing here but a few bugs."

"Those I can live with." She dropped her pack, then spread out a blanket before seating herself. "I think we'll be safe here tonight. What was wrong with the vase?"

"It had a hidden microphone in it. Someone figured out where we were and was trying to listen in. I doubt they could hear much. Our voices were too far away and too low. I don't know if there was anything else in there but Dad will look."

She nodded, barely able to see him in the dimness of the light. He sat beside her, his arm around her drawing her close. "Sleep, my love. We'll need to move on in the early morning. I hate this for you."

She yawned, then patted his chest. "It's okay, Nigel. I'm willing to do this to keep you safe. If it means too that my town is freed, then I'll gladly do this." She slept, tight in his arms, feeling safe for the first time in days.

Nigel sighed. It was going to be a long night. He knew he would doze off and on but not sleep long or hard. Things were heating up. He checked his phone. Just a few bars. He sent off a text to Nevin, letting him know what had happened and telling him he'd be back in touch when they found somewhere to hide that was safe.

His head raised as he heard a sound and drew in his breath sharply, then relaxed again. He wasn't used to being on this end of things, of protecting someone. That was others' responsibility.

Chapter 11

Havan stirred early the next morning, for a moment not sure where she was. She reached for Nigel, not finding him and then panicking. She jumped to her feet and made her way to the cave entrance, finding him crouched there, his attention on the deer trail. He reached a finger to still her question and then drew her back into the cave.

His lips close to her ear, he asked, "Is there another way out of here? They've tracked us."

She nodded, working rapidly to repack what little they had taken out of their packs, and then reaching for his hand to lead him back into the cave, to a tunnel that lead upwards. They finally stood on a hill, looking down at the trail, sheltered by the trees. Nigel looked around, finding a large rock and rolling it towards the exit, struggling with it. He turned as he felt Havan's touch and saw her pointing to some brush.

"Use this. It will stop them long enough for us to get away, if they do find the cave."

"Good thinking." He straightened up, stretching, then hugging her. "Where to now?"

She turned in a circle. "This way. It will lead us towards home, but not take us the full way. There're more caves we can use if we have to." She stared up at him. "Send a text to your family. You may not have enough bars or whatever it is you call them later on."

He nodded, pulling out his phone to send off a text, hesitating as he read one from Nolan. "Nolan's heading for your home. He and Angus. Your father apparently said something that has started them off on a search of some kind."

She frowned. "Oh, those papers he hid. I never thought about them. He's been gathering information for years now. That's likely what they're after. They won't find it at the cabin. Tell them to head for Josh. He knows where Dad hid it."

Nigel nodded, his fingers flying across the phone before he pocketed it and hugged her again. "Lead on, general. Let's see where we end up."

She nodded, not catching his attempt at teasing her. He shrugged, shouldering his pack and setting off after her. Somehow, he prayed the Lord would protect them but he had fears, fears that would be realized before the day would be over.

Havan stopped finally, pointed to a sheltered area. She dropped her pack and sank to the ground, reaching for a bottle of water.

"We're about five miles from the cabin. I won't take us there. There's an abandoned mill not far from here or some abandoned cabins we can hole up in if we have to."

He nodded, swallowing the mouthful of water he had taken, listening to the sounds of the woods around them. So far, nothing had seemed off, but he knew it was just an illusion. Things could change on a dime, and he had seen that too many times. Not quite thirty, he had worked in the family business off and on since he was a teenager, going full time after he graduated from college.

Noise came at them from the trail and they shrank back, hiding as much as they could. They watched the men walk past them and stared at one another. How had they found them? Nigel pointed to the packs and shook his head. They had to leave them.

Somehow they must have put in a tracking device he thought. He frowned, pulling off his shoes and then taking Havan's. They were fine.

He pulled her to her feet and mouth close to her ear whispered that they had to leave the packs, to take what they could of the food and water and move on. She nodded, sighing as she did so. So much for being safe. Lord, please? Get us out of here. I can't do this. Not any more.

She followed Nigel this time, letting him lead for a while, her hand on his arm directing him silently when he hesitated. She partially turned as she heard a noise behind her, an arm wrapping around her from behind and a hand closing off the scream breaking from her.

Nigel spun, seeing Havan in the arms of one of the men who had been at the cabin and sprang towards them, going down under the blow from the side of the trail. He crumpled to the ground, not seeing Havan's struggles to escape or how her hands were bound in front of her, or the cruel way she was shoved past him, her eyes on him, praying he was alive and would find her. She was suddenly terrified, having never experienced anything like this before and never dreaming this would happen.

A few minutes later, Nolan knelt by his brother, rolling him over and assessing him. Nigel flinched as he touched his head.

"Havan. They took her. That way." He pointed towards the east. "Find her, Nolan. Bring her back. Please."

Nolan nodded as he stood, seeing the tears on his brother's cheeks, tears he knew Nigel was not aware he was shedding. He had never heard the sobs in Nigel's voice either. He spoke quietly to Angus and Charlie and then ran towards the direction Nigel had pointed at. He knew he was only a few minutes behind her and prayed he could free her without her being hurt.

He crouched at the top of the hill, watching as the two men argued, Havan sitting off to the side, her head turning as she struggled with her bonds. He looked around, then moved quietly through the underbrush towards her. Just as he was near her, he stopped, his eyes on the men and their argument, which was growing louder and almost to the point of violence. He shook his head. He crept forward, a hand around Havan's mouth, an arm around her body, and pulled her back with him, closing the underbrush behind them before he grabbed her arm and hurried her away, his head turned slightly.

Good, he thought. So far, we're fine. He stopped suddenly, shoving her behind a tree and covering her with his body, his head burrowed in his arms. He heard the men running back towards Nigel and prayed that the three men there had disappeared. He looked down at Havan and frowned. She was angry, he could tell. Reaching for his knife, he sliced through the rope, freeing her hands.

She held up a finger, her head tilted as she listened, then grabbing his hand, ran towards the west, away from where they had been heading. She finally stopped, leaning against a large rock, gulping in air. He slid to the ground, his chest heaving as well. She sat beside him, her eyes on him.

"Nigel? Is he okay?"

"He'll have a headache, but he's fine. Angus and Charlie are with him. They'll get him to safety. Just where, they'll let me know. Where are we heading? This isn't the way to the cabin."

She shook her head. "That's where they think we'll head. I'm heading away from there, towards another town. Hopefully, we can make it and find somehow to get to your parents."

"We'll make it, Havan. Somehow or other, we'll make it." He stood, assessing the area around him. "I think we're safe for now. Which way now?"

"This way."

Two hours later, she stopped at the edge of a town, searching around. It was getting dark, and she needed to find the building she wanted before night fell. Nolan pulled her back. "Let me call for help. Is there an address they can find us at?"

She rattled it off, then headed away from the downtown area. She finally drew him into an abandoned house, listening carefully for any sounds, breathing a sigh of relief at hearing none. "We'll be safe here for a bit, I pray. How long for them to reach us?"

"Fifteen minutes at the most. Your father sent them this way, knowing you'd head for here."

Nolan pulled her with him about ten minutes later, recognizing the vehicle, shoving her into the back seat and sliding in after her, pushing her down to the seat.

"Stay hidden for now, Havan. We're heading out of here, but I don't want you to be seen. Chances are they've figured out the plates on all our vehicles."

"They likely have." Nevin spoke from the front seat, sharing a look with his father, who drove. "We're heading home."

"Home? Not back to the house?" Nolan was surprised.

"No. Not there. We need to have better security on these two, and that house has been compromised in some way. Joe did a sweep and found some interesting items."

Nolan groaned. "So, how?"

"Cleaners. They admitted they let a utility man in the other day, thinking we had okayed it."

Havan listened to the men before her thoughts shifted. Something was still off about all this. She just wasn't sure what. She placed a hand on Nolan's arm, bringing his attention back to him.

"Who were the cleaners?"

When Nixon named them, she nodded, the men catching her movement in the light from the dash. Nolan had finally let her sit back upright.

"They're related to the mayor, but not close to him. One of them hates him in fact. So, who would they be working for? And the utility man? Can you get a description of him?”

“Better than that. I have a picture.” Nevin passed his phone back to her.

“That’s the mayor himself. He’s bold, I must say. He’s that desperate?”

Nevin nodded, his eyes on her face as he took his phone. “He is. He’s vowing to get to you, Havan. And Nigel. He knows he’s lost out on the money. It’s gone to a charity now. He’ll never have a chance at it. He’s on the run from the moneylenders himself as well. He’ll make a mistake and we’ll catch him.”

“Before or after I die?” She turned to stare out the window, not catching the shocked look the three men exchanged.

“You’re sure Nigel is okay?” Her voice was low, almost pleading with Nolan as she turned to him.

“He’s fine, Havan. He has a headache but Angus and Charlie are almost home with him. He’ll be looked at and then be waiting for when we get there.” Nevin turned to watch her face, seeing something in it that had him frowning. He would have to talk to Nigel, but somehow he knew Havan had made a decision to fight the mayor and not sit back any more.

Havan ran for the house the moment Nolan helped her from the vehicle, finding her father waiting, arms open to hug her. They clung to one another for a moment before Jackson set her back from her.

"You're okay, Havan?"

"I'm fine, Dad. The wrists are sore, but other than that, I'm okay physically."

"But you're mad. I can see that." He watched her closely as she finally nodded. "Don't let your anger lead you to do something you'll regret."

"I won't, Dad. I promise." She looked around, not seeing her husband. "Nigel?"

"Upstairs, love. Third door on your right." His hand stopped her. "He's fine, Havan. A sore head, a bruise with some bleeding. But he's fine."

She nodded, reaching up to kiss her father's cheek before she ran for the stairs. She had to see for herself. She paused at the door before quietly opening it and entering, searching for Nigel, sighing as she found him already asleep. She stood for a few minutes, her eyes on him before she turned. She desperately needed a shower. She would thank Naomi in the morning for the clothes. She knew it was likely her. Then she paused, her eyes turning to the closed bathroom door, as she touched the clothes on the counter. No, she thought. Nigel would have taken care of that, even if he had had to have his mother buy them for her.

She stood once more by the bed, hesitating before she slipped in beside her husband, her hand coming out to his shoulder. She needed that contact with him, to know he was still with her. Thank you, Lord, was all she could manage before she slept.

She didn't hear the quiet tap at the door or her name called before Naomi opened the door, a tray of food in her hands, Nixon behind her. Naomi stood for a moment, her eyes on the younger couple, before she turned, Nixon taking the tray from her, and closing the door. They needed sleep, she decided, more than they needed food.

Chapter 12

Early the next morning, Nigel stirred, rising before he realized that Havan was there. He stood, his eyes on her, before he dressed and left to find his father. He needed to talk to him. He had an idea of how to stop the hunt now and wanted to run it by his father.

Nixon listened, his eyes watchful, asking questions as needed. "Let me think on it, son. It's an ambitious plan but may work. I'll need a day." He pointed to his son. "Keep your wife away from the door. She's ready to run after the mayor and stop this right now. We can't have her doing that."

Nigel stopped pacing his eyes on his father. "What makes you say that?"

"Just something in her face last night. Nolan wants to talk to you but he's already headed for the office. We're planning on keeping you two here for now." Nixon nodded towards the windows. "Stay inside as much as possible. I know how hard that will be on Havan. She loves the outdoors."

Nigel turned again to the door before stopping, his head turned slightly. "We need to go on the offensive, Dad. No more sitting around waiting for something to happen. We need to be the ones making it happen."

"That is what we're working on, son. Just take care of your wife. That's your job right now."

Nigel left without speaking, heading for the stairs and his wife. He needed to see for himself she was all right. He hesitated at the door, his head going down, his eyes closing in prayer. He didn't see Nora standing watching him. She had come to find him, wanting to talk to him. She turned and walked away, knowing now was not the time. It might never be the time, she thought. Lord, I'm so sorry. My mouth got me into trouble again, and this time hurt my family in a way it shouldn't have.

Nigel shut the door quietly behind him, not seeing Havan at all. He searched. No, she was not in the bedroom. Now, where would she be?

He turned, hearing a slight noise, and walking to the large closet. He stood for a moment, watching Havan, before he reached and pulled her to him. She clung to him, her tears soaking his shirt.

"Nigel, I was so afraid. I thought they had killed you." She finally looked up at him.

"They tried. But it was you they wanted, my love. How do we keep you safe?"

She shrugged, her head going back on his chest, hearing the strong beat of his heart, knowing he loved her and would protect her in any way that he could. "I don't know, Nigel. We just can't sit back."

He smiled at how nearly matched to his own words hers were. "I talked to Dad. He's working on a plan. But we can't have you running off on your own, my love."

"I know." She moved away from him, heading for the bathroom and a warm washcloth to wash her face, once again. She had lost count of the times already this morning. This was not her, to weep like this.

Nigel finally sat her down, an arm around her. "We need to talk, Havan. Dad wants us to stay here for a few days. It's up to you. We can stay or we can go to my place."

She watched him, not wanting to make the decision. "What is your choice?"

"My choice? It would be to go home. We'd have personnel there, but we'd be alone. We need that time. We never did get to our talks we wanted to have.”

“I would like that, Nigel. That way we’d not be putting your parents at risk.” She paused, biting at her lip. “We need to talk to Dad too. I saw him briefly last night when I got here.”

“We’ll do that. But first, let’s spend some time in prayer. We need that.”

An hour later, the young couple drove away, without seeing their family. They had decided just to leave a note, not wanting an argument. Nixon went looking for them a hour after that, finding the note and then running for his office, calling for Nolan and Nevin who were there.

“They’ve left.” Nevin stared at his father. “Back to Nigel’s?”

“That’s what they said. Get men over there now. It looks like they had an hour head start.” Nixon reached for his phone, relieve to hear Nigel’s voice. “Nigel?”

“We’re safe, Dad. We’re at home. We need this.”

“I know you do. But I wish you had talked to me first.”

"Why? So you could talk us out of this?" Nigel abruptly hung up, leaving Nixon staring at his phone.

"He hung on you?" Nolan shook his head, before laughing. "Well, then, that settles it. Let's go, Nevin. We need to talk some sense into him."

Nixon held up a hand. "Wait, guys. Let's make some plans before you two hotheads go over there."

Havan stared at Nigel, horrified. "You just hung up on your Dad."

"I know." He sighed. "I should't have. I'll call him later. But right now, you're my priority." He reached to pull her closer to him where they sat on the couch in the sunroom. "I haven't had near enough time to cuddle with my best lady."

She shook her head at him. "And just how much time will we have before they head over?"

"Not enough." He laughed at the look on her face, before reaching a hand to touch her cheek. "You are so beautiful, and you don't even know it, do you?"

"No, I've never thought of myself that way. Never had competition with other girls." She tilted her head. "You've never shaved your beard off. I thought your Mom said you were always clean shaven."

"I was. But a certain wife has decided she likes the look, or so she says."

She snorted. "Blame me, sure." She searched the sky through the large windows. "Nigel, what are we to do? He's out there. You can be sure he'll find us again."

"I know he will. I just pray we have a plan in place to protect you before he does, but he seems to be moving quickly."

Nigel finally rose as he heard the door bell, regret in his heart that their time had been interrupted. He checked, then swung the door open. Nolan and Charlie entered, Nolan's eyes searching his brother's face before he grinned.

"Tried to pull a fast one, did you?"

Nigel shrugged, not willing to comment. "How long was it before you found out?"

"Dad said about an hour. How did you ever manage to get away without the guys seeing you?"

Nigel frowned. "I have no idea. They should have stopped us." The brothers shared a look and then turned to Charlie, who was already on the phone. Something had gone wrong there and they had to find out who had failed.

"Where's Havan?"

"Either the sunroom or the library. We were in the sunroom but she wanted to check out the library. Nolan, we need this over and soon. This is wearing her down. She's not used to living like this."

"I know, Nigel. We're trying to come up with a plan, but every time we do, something happens. It's like they're reading our minds."

Nolan froze. "I think he is. Somehow, he is. But how?"

"He's tracking us. He has someone following us. He's watching your family, Nolan." Havan spoke from where she stood behind Nigel in the hallway. "Come on out to the kitchen. I'm hungry and I get grumpy when I'm hungry."

"When you're tired too." Nigel dodged the swat aimed at him before turning her and walking with her to the kitchen, Nolan following.

"Nolan, where's Nora?" Havan spun from where she was working at the counter.

"She was at Dad's earlier. I'm not sure where now. Why?"

"Because I want to talk to her. She needs to understand she did hurt me but I forgive her. We need to get along, don't we, if we're family now?"

Nigel and Nolan shared a long look, Nigel shaking his head finally at Nolan.

"We'll find her, love. Just not right at this moment." Nigel rose to take the plates of sandwiches from her, dropping a kiss on her cheek as she did so, causing a faint blush to rise. He grinned down at her before he sobered and set their plates on the breakfast bar, waiting for her to seat herself before he sat back down.

"What now, Nolan? Surely you've come up with a plan."

He laughed. "That's what I like about you, Havan. Direct and to the point." He wiped his fingers on the napkin she had handed him. "We're working on one. This place is fine for now, but be prepared to move if we need to do that. It may be sudden."

She nodded. "Any idea on where he is now?"

Nolan shook his head. "He's gone undercover. Joe's been back to Sanctuary.

No one has seen him." He frowned, remembering his conversation with Joe. "In fact, his family seem to have disappeared too."

She snorted. "Of course, they would. Maybe now they'll have freedom to live."

"What do you mean?" Nigel was watching her face.

"I mean, they had no freedom. They had to toe the line, so to speak. Even his wife had to obey what he said. You could see it in their mannerisms, their demeanour. Someone reported him years ago, but nothing came from that. Dad and Josh suspected he paid off the official."

Nolan pulled out his phone, reading the text quickly. "They found Andy. He was knocked out and bound. Someone pretended to be him when you left. That means they know where you are now."

Nigel gave a sound of frustration, his arm around Havan. "How did they get the drop on Andy?"

"We don't know yet. He's still out and on his way to the hospital. I never noticed he wasn't there. That means whoever was pretending to be him was still there when we left." He was on his feet, heading for the hallway. "Charlie! We've got big problems!"

Havan shrank back against Nigel. "Nigel?"

"I know, love, I know. We need to find a spot to tuck you away for the next little while. But where?"

"I'm not leaving you. I refuse to."

Nigel nodded, his attention going to the hallway where he heard the two men talking. "I'll be right back."

Havan listened to the conversation as she cleared away their dishes, leaving their mugs where they were. She was suddenly deeply terrified, knowing the mayor had taken this step. Then she paused. No, it wasn't the mayor. He didn't have the resources or the smarts for this.

"Nigel?" She approached the men, causing them to turn. "What if it's not the mayor? What if it's whoever is after him? Using us to get him to come out into the open?"

Nolan was on his phone, calling for help, knowing they might not get there in time. Charlie and Nigel ran to lock the house up. Havan spun to go and help, Nolan's hand on her arm keeping her in place.

She turned to him as he pocketed his phone. "We have help coming, but they might not make it in time. Where can we put you?"

She shrugged. "I don't know the house. You do." She heard a sound from the outside. "Nolan? Where's Nigel?"

"Locking up. Come on. To the basement. We'll stay there. Nigel and Charlie will find us."

There was the sound of breaking glass and smoke began to fill the hallway. Nolan grasped her hand pulling her towards the basement before he fell, taking her with him, gloved hands reaching to pull the two of them up and out of the house and shoving them into a van. Blindfolded and gagged quickly, their hands were bound. Havan slumped back on the seat. Nigel? Please be okay? Lord, protect me.

Nixon and Nevin ran for the door to Nigel's home, seeing it open, fear running through their hearts. The smoke had cleared by the time they had arrived. They searched, finding Nigel and Charlie unconscious.

"Where are Nolan and Havan?" Nevin spun in a circle. "They should be here."

"Search the house and then call for help. This has become worse than we thought."

Nevin and Nixon finally stood, men from their team standing around them, as they watched the stretchers with Nigel and Charlie laying on them removed from the house. Nixon was afraid, more afraid than he had ever been. He had received word on the way over that it was not the mayor after Havan. It was the moneylender who Brown owed so much to.

"What now, Dad?" Nevin spoke his thoughts aloud, knowing his father would not have thought through a plan as yet.

"We pray and pray hard, son. Pray that they contact us and not Brown."

Nigel nodded, knowing that possibility was unlikely.

Chapter 13

Nolan listened carefully as they drove away, trying to pick up any words, any sounds that would help him identify their captors and hearing nothing. He finally gave up, knowing he couldn't get them out of where they were right then. He would wait and then find a way to get Havan away. He could feel her beside him, crammed in as they were. He knew she was angry, he could sense that from her.

Havan was terrified but also very angry. She was getting tired of this. She just wanted to live her life with her new husband and that didn't seem to be the plan right now. Lord, now what? I know You're here and in control. But, Lord, captive again? What's the purpose of that? Please, dear Lord, protect Nigel. If I don't make it back, please comfort him. Let him know how much I love him. She stopped, sensing the car had halted.

They were pulled roughly from the vehicle and shoved into a building. Nolan hit the floor on hands and knees as he was shoved roughly into a room. He spun, reaching for the blindfold, his hands stilling as he felt a weapon against his neck and then the ropes binding his hands was cut. He heard the door slam shut and locked.

He reached for the blindfold and the gag, blinking in the pale light that came through the dirt-encrusted windows. He rose, brushing at the dirt on his knees before he began a systemic search of the room, not finding anything that would help him identify where he was. He felt his pocket. They had left his phone. He looked for a place to hide it, finding a small crack that would fit it just right. But where was Havan?

He stood, ear to the door, not hearing anything. Where was she? Lord, please keep her safe.

Havan spun around from where she had been shoved into a room beside Nolan's, waiting for what, she wasn't sure. Her hands freed, she waited, not reaching for the blindfold or gag, knowing someone was still in the room with her. She tilted her head as she heard soft movements before her arm was taken gently and she was moved to a chair, her blindfold and gag removed. She refused to open her eyes.

"It's okay, Havan. They've left."

Her eyes opening, she stared in disbelief at the mayor's wife.

"What? What are you doing here? Janet Brown?"

Janet nodded. "I sent the girls away. Ed has been so wrong, but I couldn't tell him that. He's just refused to listen. What he did to you two was so wrong. I told him that, waited until he left, and then packed up the girls and left. I was grabbed two days ago when I was out shopping. I have no idea who the men were."

Havan rubbed her arms. "I think I know. Did you know your husband is highly in debt to a moneylender?"

Janet shook her head. "I suspected that. I knew he was spending more money than he earned. I wish I had never heard of Sanctuary. But he insisted we move there. Again, I have no idea why."

"I know. Did you know he was to inherit millions if his daughters married by a certain date? The oldest one's date just passed. When she missed it, that meant they all missed it." Havan watched with compassion as Janet shook her head, sorrow on her face.

"I heard what he did to you and your husband. That was so wrong. I told him that."

"And paid the price, didn't you?" Havan's hand gently touched the bruises on the older woman's cheek. "I have to forgive him, I must in order to live. Nigel is not the first of my family he hurt."

Janet stared at her. "But what do you mean? It's just been your father and you."

Havan nodded, knowing her next words would totally destroy the woman. "My mother was really sick when I was tiny. Dad couldn't get her into the doctor or get the doctor to her. Your husband's men prevented that."

"And then she died." Janet rose to her feet and began to pace. "I knew he had developed a black heart. I just never knew it was so dark. He wasn't like that when we married. He was a good man, at least I thought he was." She turned to Havan, coming back to sit beside her. "Tell me, Havan. Do you believe?"

Havan nodded. "I do. So does Nigel and his complete family."

"Then, help me get back to where I need to be. I have tried but I fear I have lost some of the sparkle of my faith. The girls know and believe but are so afraid of their father."

"They're safe?"

Janet nodded. "They are. A friend took them somewhere, where Ed can't find them. He doesn't know this friend."

"That's good." Havan listened for a moment to the footsteps pacing outside the room. "We're in a pickle here, Janet. Somehow we need to get away. If you get a chance, run. Look for Nigel's family. Tell them where we are."

Janet finally nodded. "Who did they bring with you? I know you weren't alone."

Havan shook her head. "I won't say, Janet. It's too dangerous. I have no idea who may be listening in on us. It's a given that someone is."

Janet stared at her, shocked. "Listening in? How can that be?"

Havan simply shook her head, knowing that if she named Nolan, he was as good as dead. Lord, protect him and get him back to his family. I don't care about me. Comfort Nigel, please, if I don't.

Nolan listened to the quiet voices from the room next door, puzzled as to who was with Havan. It was a feminine voice, he knew. But who? Lord, protect her. Send her home safely to Nigel. Protect our family, please Lord. Lead them to us.

He finally sank to the floor, his head back against the wall, listening for what, he wasn't sure. He heard movement from the room beside him, knowing that meant Havan was still alive and well. His eyes sought the crack where he had hidden his phone, knowing his family would be trying to trace him. Bring them quickly, Lord, before something happens that shouldn't.

Havan finally sank to the floor in a corner, her knees drawn up, her face down on her folded arms. She had moved away from Janet, not sure she could trust her. Something was saying not to. She had learned to trust that voice inside her. She turned her head slightly so she could watch Janet without being noticed and frowned. What was she up to? She had pulled something from her pocket and was tapping away. She had been right, after all. Janet was a plant. Now how to use that to her advantage? Lord, I'm out of ideas. Please provide some.

Janet finally tucked her phone away. Her girls were safe, that was all that mattered.

She knew Havan had been watching her, she had felt her eyes. She just couldn't let her know she was only checking on her girls. Lord, Havan says You're still there. Please, Lord, bring me back to Your sanctuary. To the city where I can be safe, where my girls can be too.

Hours later, the door was unlocked and a tray slid in. Havan stared at Janet, who nodded.

"That's how we get our food. We don't see who it is. If they come in, we stand with our faces to the wall."

"This is so wrong, Janet. We're human beings with feelings, dreams, hopes. Not some animal to be treated like this."

Janet shook her head. "It's how they do it, Havan. They treat us like this. Again, I have no idea as to who they are or what they want."

"Your husband. That's who. They took me because they'll use me to draw him out and here, knowing how much he wants to kill me."

"Kill you?" Janet's shocked look startled Havan for a moment before she nodded.

"He does. I heard his men talking when he took me only yesterday, was it? He's angry, beyond mad, that I prevented him marrying your oldest to Nigel. That kept him from getting millions. He had planned to pay off his debts and then disappear."

"Disappear? He would never do that." Janet stared at Havan, seeing the compassion Havan felt for her. "Disappear? Where?"

Havan shrugged, before sliding down against the wall, her hand behind her, idly tapping on the wall Janet thought.

Nolan listened as he heard the taps, then grinned. Morse Code. Old school, but something he and his brothers had enjoyed when they were younger, pretending to be spies and detectives and whatever their imagination made them. He tapped back, listening for her response. He breathed a sigh of relief. She was safe, but had the mayor's wife with her. Now, what was up with that?

He moved away from the wall after a while, standing at the window, scraping away at the dirt so he could look out. He wasn't familiar with the area, but maybe Havan was. He just knew they had driven around for at least two hours. That would have been enough time to get back into Havan's home area.

He stayed where he was when the door opened. He heard movement behind him and then a voice asking him where the mayor was?

He shook his head. "I have no idea. I haven't seen him. Check with his family. They should know where he it."

He waited until he heard the footsteps retreat and the door lock behind the man. He frowned. This is bizarre. Obviously it's not the mayor who had taken them. It had to be the ones he owed the money to. Now what, he wondered. He walked over to examine the door, feeling in his pocket for his knife. He still had it. These men had not searched them at all. That was concerning and a red flag. It meant they had no intention of letting them get away. Nigel, I'm sorry. I tried. Please forgive me.

Chapter 14

Sitting on the side of the emergency room stretcher, an oxygen mask on his face, Nigel wiped at the tears still coming to his eyes. Whatever the smoke had been, it had really affected his vision for the moment. Nixon said Charlie was up and about, not as affected as Nigel.

"Dad?" He pulled the oxygen mask away for a moment. "Any word?"

Nixon shoved the mask back onto his son's face, a frown in place as he saw the tear tracks through the black on his son's face. "Not yet. We're working on something. Nolan's phone is still active so Angus is tracking that. But we have no idea if he had it when they got wherever it is they are."

"Where are they, Dad?"

Nixon shook his head. "We're working on it, Nigel. We've got the authorities moving in on where Nolan's phone is. They're waiting on their tactical officers."

"I want to be there." Nigel moved to slide off the stretcher, then stopped as his head spun.

"No, you're not, Nigel. You're under treatment and I will not let you walk out of here until you're cleared to go. Understand that?"

Nigel finally nodded, sliding back on the stretcher to lay down. His eyes slid closed as he prayed as he hadn't prayed in a while. Somewhere out there was his wife and his brother and no one knew exactly where.

Four long days passed without finding the two. The officers had found Nolan's phone and evidence that they had been there in the building but not them. What had puzzled them was evidence of a second woman. No one knew who it was.

"Who was there with them, Dad?" Nevin paced their security office, Nigel sprawled in a chair nearby, his head back, eyes closed. Charlie's eyes watched Nigel, regret in them, that he hadn't been able to prevent what had happened.

"That's what we're trying to figure out. Any thoughts?"

"Brown's wife." Nigel raised his head, a bleak look on his face.

"His wife? What makes you say that?" Nevin sat on the edge of his father's desk, folding his arms across his chest, watching his brother closely.

"They'll go after whoever they can to reach him. I have no idea what state his marriage is in and frankly don't care, but they'll go after his family. What about his daughters?"

"Now, that's interesting." Nixon leaned back in his chair, tapping his pen on his other hand. "They've disappeared completely. It seems once Brown left town, so did his wife and daughters. We have a place where she was seen about a week ago, but no sign of the daughters."

"She's put them into hiding somewhere. Smart lady." Nigel stared at the floor, missing the looks sent his way. "He's used them enough to try and forward his plans."

Nevin rose once more to pace. "He has at that. Any word on the moneylender, Dad?"

"No, not at all. That's concerning. He was seen in Sanctuary about five days ago and then not since."

"Five days? Then it was his men, not the mayor's that took us?"

"That's what Brett thinks. He's working that angle for me, tracking anything he can." He looked up as Brett appeared in the doorway. "Brett? You have word?"

"I might. We need Jackson here. Where is he?"

"At the house." Charlie was on his feet. "I'll be back with him in thirty minutes max."

The three men waited, looking up as Jackson almost ran into the room.

"You have word?" He sagged when they shook their heads, waving him to a chair.

"What we need from you is whatever information you can give us on the wife and daughters of the mayor."

"Not a lot, I'm afraid. They were seldom seen in town. He never let them roam the town. They had tutors for the girls, he didn't want them mingling with the townsfolk or the outsiders." He looked at Nixon, eyes keen with knowledge. "Let me guess. His girls are missing and so's his wife."

"That they are. We think she's hidden the girls somewhere and that she may also be held by the same men who have Havan and Nolan."

Jackson slowly nodded. "I would think they'd take his wife, but that won't help them.

He had nothing but contempt for her. She was battered emotionally, I would say. Not physically. Emotional, mental, whatever you want to call it. I saw her about a month ago. She looked scared but there was something different about her. I think she was planning on leaving as soon as an opportunity came up." He rose to pace, hands locked behind him. "This doesn't help us find our two, though." He stopped, staring at the painting on the wall, a frown in place. "Who has them, Nix?"

"We think the moneylender does. We're still watching the mayor."

Jackson turned to watch Nixon as he spoke, before his eyes caught movement on Nigel's part. Lord, he's hurting in more ways than one. First his wife, then his brother. Bring them home safe, please, dear Lord. If not, comfort us.

Nevin looked around from where he had seated himself, catching movement outside the door and then rising to go speak with Angus before he spun to stare back through the door. Hurried words carried on, and then Angus was on the run, heading for a vehicle and Nevin was headed to his own office, booting up his computer and doing a search before he was on his feet, reaching for the papers on the printer, and running for his father's office.

"Dad? We found them."

Nigel was on his feet, his hand on his brother's arm. "Where?"

"The old mill outside Sanctuary. Someone reported suspicious activity around it and the county force sent some officers. They're waiting for us. Angus has gone to the airport, readying our copter."

Nigel was at the door as he heard his father's voice. "Nigel, wait. We need to pray first and foremost. We have no idea what we're walking into."

Nigel turned, nodding, impatient as he was to go, knowing his father was right. They needed God to lead them. That was the only way to go, and he had been forgetting that, worry for Havan driving him to a lack of sleep and not enough to eat. His mother had been forcing him to sit down to a meal, but he just picked at it, drinking instead the tea she kept setting in front of him.

They finally landed near the town of Sanctuary, vehicles waiting for them. Nigel listened as his father spoke with the officers, his eyes on his son.

"Nigel, we need you to stay back. Charlie and Joe will be with you at all times." Nevin waited until Nigel nodded. "They'll go after you if they have realized they have the wrong man. But somehow, I doubt they've made that realization. Not yet, anyway."

Nigel stood, leaning back against the car, his eyes on the path the men had taken, his heart breaking that she might not be there after all. They couldn't tell them for sure that they were.

He heard the shouts of the law enforcement officers, then the banging of wood on wood, and then a shot. He stood abruptly, ready to run forward, but Charlie stepped in his way, shaking his head.

"Wait, Nigel. They'll come for us when they want us."

Nigel sighed, slumping back, knowing Charlie was right, his eyes on the path once more. He heard running feet and saw Nevin heading his way.

"Nevin?"

"We have them, Nigel, but they're hurt. Dad wants you back at the copter. We're heading back home. They'll bring in an air ambulance for them."

"Wait. Nevin. How bad?" Nigel's hand clenched onto his brother's arm.

"I don't know. They're alive, Nigel. That much I know. The reason for the air support is to get them out of here and to safety as quickly as we can."

Nigel nodded, his eyes still searching the path, willing Havan to walk towards him, even though he had just been told she wouldn't. "You're sure, Nevin?"

"I am, Nigel. Dad's seen them and came back out to talk to me. He hasn't said much, so I can't tell you much more than that." He didn't tell his brother that when asked about Havan, Nixon's face had hardened and become grim. Nevin knew then she was badly hurt.

Chapter 15

Nigel paced the waiting room in the emergency room of their local hospital, willing the physician to come out. No one had been near them and that frustrated him, as much as he knew they were still assessing them.

"Nigel, you need to sit." His mother stood in his way, her hands reaching out to grasp his arms.

"I can't sit still, Mom. Not until I know what's going on with her."

"I know that, son, but wearing yourself out won't help." She threw a helpless look at Nixon, who just shook his head, knowing if it was him, he would be pacing too.

Jackson sat, head back against the wall, eyes closed in prayer. He knew they would be out soon to talk to them. He wanted to be prepared. He looked up as he heard commotion near him.

Amy almost ran towards the physician as he called her name, Nixon and Naomi right behind her, before she followed him. She stood for a moment, staring at her husband before reaching for his hand, causing his eyes to open. She saw the pain in them and frowned.

"Nolan? Are you okay, sweetheart?"

He nodded. "I am, darling. Broken leg and all, but I'm fine."

"Broken leg? Nolan! How?"

He looked past them at his parents, his eyes lingering on his father's face, who nodded. "I tried to stop them from hurting Havan. One of them kicked me as I was moving, right in the lower leg. Snapped one of the bones."

Amy touched his face, bringing his eyes back to her. "What happened, Nolan?"

"Not now, Amy. I still have to give my statement, so they don't want me saying anything." He touched her cheek. "I'm just glad to be home."

He watched as she finally walked away with his mother before turning to his father. "They tried to kill Havan, Dad. That's why I tried to stop them."

"Figured it was something like that. We haven't heard how she is, yet. We'll talk and soon. I know the officers are waiting outside for your statement. Tell them to come get Amy when they're done."

Nolan nodded as he gripped his father's hand before Nixon walked away, anger burning inside him. Anger that he needed to tamp down before he found Nigel.

Nigel finally stood at Havan's bedside, his hand on hers, watching as her head tossed slightly. He frowned at the bandage around her head, the bruising forming on her face. Jackson stood on her other side, mindful of the equipment and the IV line running to her arm.

"Nigel?"

"I want those men, Jackson. They've hurt her and the physicians aren't even sure just how much."

"I know, son. They've said they're keeping her sedated for now, letting her rest. They're concerned about her eyesight, are they not?"

Nigel nodded. "They said something about it not being right. Does that mean she can't see?"

"For now, it does, Mr. Wells." A voice behind him startled Nigel and had him turning.

A female physician stood there, her eyes on Havan, before she moved in to assess her.

"Doctor? What do you mean?"

"I mean, that for now, for some reason she can't see. There is some swelling near the optic nerve, which is causing us concern. That's why we want her to be as still as she can. She also may have seen something that has caused this."

"Something? Like what?"

"That you would have to ask her. She may have buried it though, if it's too painful for her to remember."

"Will she ever?"

The physician shrugged. "That's hard to say. We can't tell you she will. We can't tell you she won't." Her eyes studied Nigel for a moment. "She'll be here for four or five days, long enough for us to run a number of tests. Then, you can take her home."

"Understand something, doctor. I will not leave her side, not for any reason. You will never ask me to go home. It's not happening."

She started to speak, to deny him that before she say Jackson shaking his head.

"Don't even attempt that, young lady. You may be the physician here. This here is her husband. He's the one who will have to deal with everything she's been through and will be going through. Not you. I don't want my daughter awakening in the night, all alone and not able to see. It's not happening. If he's not there, I am."

Jackson stared her down. She knew she should be denying them, but having heard what Havan had been through, she didn't have the heart to say no.

Nixon stood a while later, his eyes on his son as he sat at Havan's bedside. They had moved her to a private room on a different floor. He knew Nolan was just down the hall from her. Police officers stood at their doors and Nixon had made arrangements for some of his own men to be there as well.

He walked towards Nigel, his hand coming down on his shoulder. He had talked to Jackson, had heard what he had to say, and his heart broke for his son. It was a long road, he feared, that they would have to walk. The physician had not guaranteed she would ever see again.

"Nigel?" Nixon's voice was quiet. "What can I get you?"

"Dad? You're here? How's Nolan?"
Nigel squinted in the light, not sure what time
it even was.

"He's sleeping. Amy said the pain's
not bad. He'll be in a cast for about six weeks
and then have therapy. He's mad he couldn't
stop them. He tried his best."

"Has he said what happened over the
last four days?"

Nixon shook his head. "I haven't
talked to him yet. He gave his statement just
before they moved him up here. Amy's been
adamant that no one talk to him for a day or
so, and I must say, I agree with her. We'll
have time." He sighed, his eyes on his young
daughter-in-law. "They're still working on
gathering evidence. But it was what we
suspected. It was the moneylender. Nolan
did say he heard a name that Havan said as he
was running towards her but he can't
remember it offhand."

Nigel nodded. "Pull up a chair, Dad.
We could use your prayers." He turned as he
heard another sound and saw Nora at the
door. He rose and walked towards his sister.
"Nora? You can come in."

She searched his face, then with tears
streaming down her face, threw herself at her
brother, finding his arms coming around her

in a tight hug. "It's my fault, Nigel. If my big mouth had not been working the way it was, you two would have stayed safe."

"We don't know that for sure, Nora. He would have grabbed her anywhere he could." He studied his sister's face. "She said she forgave you, you know. She wanted to talk to you, but that's what she said."

"She did?" Nora stared, her mouth open. "That quickly?"

He nodded. "That's Havan, Nora. You need to get to know her." He paused, his eyes on the far wall, biting at his upper lip. "I don't know how she does what she does, but it's her. Just talk to her, please? That's all I ask."

Nora hugged her brother, then stepped back. "I've been going to everyone in the family. You and Havan are the last two I need to talk to. This is not the place nor the time. Call me when it is."

"Thank you, Nora." Nigel watched her walk away before he turned back to the bed, not seeing the look on his father's face.

Nixon puzzled over the words Nigel had spoken on behalf of Havan, knowing he had almost quoted her word for word. Nigel was like that, remembering words and sentences. He shook his head. This young lady had a big heart.

"Dad?"

"Yes, Nigel?" Nixon waited, knowing Nigel would speak when he was ready.

"How attached are you to the cottage?"

"The cottage? Not at all. None of us are. Why?"

"What will you charge me to buy it from you? Havan fell in love with it. It's right across the lake from her Dad's. I'd like to take her there to live."

"To live? I see. Well, son, if you want it, a dollar is all I ask." Nixon held up his hand. "That's all I want. I know you haven't been content lately working for us. You need to find where you do fit. What are your thoughts?"

Nigel shrugged. "I have no idea." He laughed. "Havan wants me to run for mayor of Sanctuary."

"That would fit, but somehow I don't think that's what you want."

Nigel shook his head. "It's not, Dad. If you could find someone to take over for me in my position, then I would gladly work in another area of the company, something I could do remotely."

"That would work. Let me think on it. I know Joe wants to move up and he's keen on the systems you've been setting up."

"He would be good. Thanks, Dad. I know that will mean a big change in the company."

"We have to adapt, son. I never asked you to come in and work for us. Neither did your mother. We want you to find the work that makes you happy, where God can use you. This is what you started out to find, wasn't it? You didn't expect to find a wife or an adventure, as they say."

"No, Dad. Neither of them. I wouldn't trade Havan for any other woman. She's the other half of my heart."

Nigel's eyes were back on Havan, watching as she slept, willing her to wake, but not wanting her to find out she couldn't see.

"How long will they keep her in?" Nixon was concerned, knowing that Nigel would want to leave for the cottage as soon as he could.

"Four days or so, from what they've told me. I'll take her back to my place here for a bit, just to let her rest." He leaned back, sighing. "Did they find the men?"

"No, and that concerns us. They could still come after her."

Nigel nodded, his thoughts not on what his father was saying. Nixon finally rose, a hand to his son's shoulder, and walked away. He had to leave him in God's hands. That was all he could do.

Nigel roused late that night, hearing Havan's restlessness, his hand on her face, stilling her movements.

"Nigel? Is that you?" Havan turned her face into his hand.

"It is, my love. You need to lie still." He watched as she frowned, then a look of pain crossed her face.

"Nigel, is it dark out? I can't see you."

"It is, love, but that's not why you can't see me." Nigel bent over her, his hands on both her cheeks, willing her to look at him.

"That's okay, then. I'll see you in the morning." She drifted off again, Nigel sighing with frustration. He had no idea how she would take the news.

Lord, help me. That was all he could pray, but he knew it would be enough.

He sat back, Havan's hand in his, as he watched his beloved wife sleep. He needed to make decisions but just couldn't. All he knew was that he had to break news to her in the morning, and he had no words to do just that.

Havan stirred in the early morning, her hand tightening on Nigel's, before her eyes opened. She frowned, seeing only minimal light, even though she could tell it was morning.

"Nigel?"

"Here, my love. How are you feeling this morning?"

"I have a horrible headache. Did you catch the men?"

"No, sorry, my love. We didn't. They were gone by the time the authorities moved in." He paused, his eyes on her, sorrow on his face at what he had to tell her.

"Why is everything so dim? I can't see your face." She reached a hand up to feel his cheek. "Did I go blind or something?"

"That's what I need to talk to you about. You are blind right now, but the doctors think it's temporary. They can't give an explanation why other than for some swelling around a nerve. You hit your head pretty hard."

"I didn't hit my head. They did. They slammed me into a rock wall, Nigel, trying to get information from me. I heard Nolan yelling at them just before I passed out." She sat up, ignoring his command to lie still. "I need out of here. He'll be coming for me."

"Who will?"

She shook her head. "I can't remember, but I know him. He's not a stranger to me. Please, Nigel, take me home."

"I can't, my love. They want to run some more tests."

She shoved at the blankets. "Take me home or I'll walk out of here on my own, and won't that be a fine sight?"

"All right. Sit still for a moment. The doctor's due around in about ten minutes. We'll talk to her."

"Talk to her all you want. I'm still leaving. Where are my clothes?"

"Havan, please. Wait. You can't get out of bed."

"Trust me. I can. I can feel my way along the wall well enough to find the closet and my clothes. If you don't help me, that's exactly what I will do."

Nigel sighed, knowing he had lost the battle. He reached into the closet, finding her clothes and handing them to her. "Do you need any help?" He pulled the curtain around the bed to give her privacy.

"With my shoes. Did you bring a sweater or T-shirt?"

"A sweater. And leggings."

"Leggings? Oh, I've never had a pair and always wanted some. This is cool. Who picked them out?"

"Nora did. She stopped by last night to see us."

"Nora? Oh, I must see her and thank her. She's just warmed my heart so much giving me these."

Opening the curtain once more, Nigel stared at her before he began to laugh. "Here, we were all worried about how you'd feel around Nora. I guess our worry was wasted."

"Nigel, when you grow up the way I did, no mother, a father who loves you dearly but is a fish out of water at times, being an outsider to your home town, having no close friends, you learn to adapt real quick. Anger and hurt feelings are wasted emotions. God impressed that on me when I was five or so. So, being angry towards your sister just doesn't wash." She pulled the sweater over her head, feeling the softness of it. "What colour?"

"A real soft yellow. It suits you. It goes well with your black hair."

"Oh, how nice." She stood, shoving her feet into shoes. "No laces. I like that. Your sister's smart. I hope you tell her that."

Nigel began to laugh again. "Havan, my love, I see you are going to turn our family upside down. How does your father deal with you?"

"He's the same way, Nigel. Losing Mom changed him in a way that most people wouldn't think could happen."

"I can see that, just by how he raised you." He turned as the door opened. "Here's the doctor, Havan. Time to face what you've done."

"Havan? Where are you going?" The doctor's voice was firm. "You're not leaving. We have tests to run today."

"Are they going to tell you anything different from yesterday? Will they bring back my sight?"

"Well, no. But we need to assess how much damage has been done and if there is any improvement."

"I'm sorry, but no more tests. No more hospital rooms. I'm leaving, whether you sign me out or not. If I have to, I'll walk out here on my own."

Nigel just shrugged as the doctor turned angry eyes on him. "She's made up her mind, and frankly, I don't blame her. She needs to be home and that I agree with. If you need tests done later in the week, I'll bring her back. But no more tests today."

The doctor finally turned on her heel. "I disagree totally with this. I'll have the nurse bring in your paperwork and the next appointments we need for you. Watch her carefully, Mr. Wells. You'll have a list of symptoms to look out for. If she develops even one, bring her back in as soon as possible."

Nigel didn't see the car following him as he drove home and into his garage. He was being followed and didn't know it. But if he had, he wouldn't have cared. All that mattered to him was Havan.

He led her carefully into the house and to the living room, sitting her on the couch, before dropping her bag near the stairs.

"We need to talk about this, Havan."

"We will, love. But can I have a cup of tea first? I didn't get my breakfast at the hospital, and really need that tea."

Nigel grinned as he shook his head. "One cup of tea coming up." He set a tray near her shortly, with tea and some toast on it. "Here's some toast as well. Right in front of you on the table. Careful. The tea's hot."

"Considering you made it with boiling water, I would expect it to be." She ate, then leaned back, her hands wrapped around her mug. "Did you eat?"

"I had a sandwich when I was getting your food." He watched as she sipped her tea, thinking she didn't need to see to eat. "Havan, now what? Where do we go with this?"

"I have no idea, Nigel. God only knows how long this will last." She squinted. "It seems a bit brighter but that could be because you have more windows here. The stairs. That I am afraid of."

"Then you only do the stairs when I'm with you." He moved over to cradle her to him, setting her mug on the table. "We do need to talk about what happened."

She sighed. "I know we do. I'm trying to remember who was there. Two of the mayor's men, two men I didn't know, and someone I know but can't remember who. It's someone I know quite well, I think."

"So it would have to be one of your neighbours. They're the only ones you know well."

"There's not that many. Four maybe that are permanent. Three or four that come and go depending on the season." She laid her head on his shoulder. "Nolan's okay?"

"He is. Amy has him home now. She brought him home in the middle of the night. He refused to stay any longer. What did you do to him that caused this rebellion? He's not been like that."

She smiled. "Losing your freedom like that does it to you. I never saw him at all when we were captive. But the mayor's wife was there. I don't trust her. She had a phone, which she shouldn't have had."

"That is disturbing. They can't find the girls."

"She said she sent them away with a friend her husband didn't know. I'm not sure how much to believe her." She yawned. "I'm sorry. I'm so tired. I didn't sleep much over the last five days or however long it has been."

"That's what Nolan said. What's this I hear about you two communicating with one another?"

"Morse code. Dad taught it to me when I was young and bored. It helped pass time in the winter."

"We had fun with that as youngsters." He knew he had to ask some hard questions, that his family needed the answer. "Work with me for a bit, Havan. Then, you can sleep. How long were you at the first place? And did you recognize anything about it?"

"We were there six or seven hours maybe? Long enough for them to feed us. Convenience store sandwiches and bottled water, but they took the labels off, so that won't help you." She thought through the four days. "Then, they took us to another house, this one more opulent than the first one. By that I mean, it was clean and had nice beds for us. A clean, well-stocked bathroom. Then they took us to the mill." She turned to look up at him, even though she couldn't see him. "The mill was near Sanctuary. I used to play in it as a kid."

"That's what we wondered. So either they made their way back there hoping to catch the mayor or someone high in the chain of command is from there.”

“I would say the latter. Don’t ask me how I know. I just do.” She gave him as many details as she could before her eyes closed and she slept.

He watched for a while before he rose, heading for his office and his computer. He needed to make notes from what she had said. He would go back over it with her, he knew, but first impressions always counted.

Chapter 16

Nigel looked up from his book as he heard Havan stirring, knowing she'd be wanting her tea. He rose, heading for the kitchen, finding her there ahead of him, her hands searching for her mug and then the tea caddy.

"Finding what you want?"

She nodded. "I am. Do you want some?"

"I could use a cup." He nodded as he said that, then realized how stupid he felt, knowing she couldn't see the nod.

"Don't beat yourself up, Nigel. I know you nodded. You always do."

He hugged her as he moved past her, reaching for the cookies his mother had dropped off. "I do, do I? Mom left some cookies if you want."

"Sounds good." She felt for a chair, pulling it back, then felt for the table to set her cup down. "I used to close my eyes when I was tiny, just to see what it was like when someone was blind and if I could manage. I hate this."

"I know you do. So do I." He perched on a chair beside her. "Havan. I've typed up what you said. We can go over it later, but do you remember anything about the man?"

She shook her head. "Other than thinking I know him well, nothing. And I don't like that. It could be anyone I know and that puts us at risk."

Nigel watched the emotions playing on her face. "Relax. Don't think about it so hard. Then, maybe you'll remember. Don't forget. You did have a head injury."

"You're such a bundle of good news, aren't you?" She sounded disgruntled, but he saw the smile playing around her mouth.

"That I am." He stood for a moment to head for his notes, sliding back into his chair.

"Whenever you're ready with that, Nigel." Havan pointed a finger at him.

"How's your sight?"

"Still foggy, but not as bad I don't think." She twisted her head to face the windows. "It seems as if it might be better, but that could just be wishful thinking."

"God will heal when you're ready, my love." He looked down at his notes, before reaching for her hand, causing her to jump. "Sorry, my love. I forgot you couldn't see my hand."

"No, it's not that, Nigel. It's just....I feel like we're near the end of whatever this is. That whoever it is will appear and it will be all over. But I'm afraid. I'm afraid he'll hurt you." She turned her face to him, a shadow on it.

"I know we are, my love. Now, I need the names of all your neighbours, their relatives and friends, if you know them."

She nodded and began to list them, stopping as they heard the doorbell. Nigel rose, heading for the door, leaving Havan sitting, her head in her hands, a puzzled look on her face.

Jackson stood outside on the porch, feeling uncomfortable, as if he was being watched, and he had no idea why.

"Jackson? Come in." Nigel stood back and then closed the door, a feeling of fright almost coursing through him. Someone was out there, he knew.

"Nigel? How is she?" Jackson's voice was low.

"Not bad. She thinks the eyesight is improving but we can't say for sure. She's slept and had her tea. Come on back to the kitchen."

Jackson's hand on his arm stopped him, and Nigel frowned at the older man. "Jackson?"

"Before we go back, I just want to thank you, Nigel. For everything." Jackson waved off Nigel's words. "She's all I have left and you've treated her like the treasure she is. Now, there's another thing. Someone has been following me. I think I know who it is, and it really disturbs me."

"Josh?" Nigel kept his voice low enough that it couldn't be heard from the kitchen.

Jackson nodded, a bleak look on his face. "Josh. There's been something off about him lately, more so than for all the years I've known him. He's been a friend, but not a close one. Because he's our next neighbour, we've visited back and forth. There's just something I can't put a finger to."

The men spun as they heard a sharp cry from Havan and ran for the kitchen. Havan was on her feet, shoving her chair back. The force of the push tumbled the chair over, taking Havan with it, her feet entangled in the legs. Her head hit the floor and she lay still.

Nigel was on his knees beside her, his hands on her head, probing for a new injury, even as Jackson removed the chair, setting it back at the table before he too dropped beside his daughter.

"Nigel?"

"She's awake, Jackson. Havan, my love, can you sit up? Here. Don't try. Let me help you." Nigel's arm was around his wife, bracing her as she leant back against him. "What happened?"

She stared at her father, seeing him clearly. "I know who it was, Dad. I know who did this to us." She turned to Nigel, sobs wracking her body.

He swept her into his arms and headed for the living room, finding his chair and cradling her to him as she wept heart-broken tears. Jackson hovered for a moment before pulling out his phone. Nigel needed Nixon here and he knew his daughter needed Naomi. Only a mother would do in this instance.

Nixon stood beside Nigel, watching as Naomi comforted Havan as only a mother could. Jackson paced, not willing to leave, but not willing to put his daughter in any more danger by being there.

"Nigel? What happened?" Nixon's voice was low.

"She remembered who was there, Dad, and when she shoved her chair back, fell. She hit her head again. I want to take her to the hospital but she's refusing to go."

"Who?" Nixon drew his son from the room, towards the office where Nevin waited. Jackson followed.

"She said Josh." Nigel stared at Jackson. "And so did you. Why?"

"I can't explain. There's just something about him I can't put my finger on. Havan is adamant he was the one there."

Nevin nodded. "That's what we've been told by the authorities. They've been watching him for the last year or so. We're pulling a lot of information on him that's not good." He sorted through the paperwork. "He's involved in a lot of shady deals lately. We think he's the moneylender and that's why Brown is so ticked off, to put it mildly, with you two, Nigel."

"What do we do then, Nevin? How do we stay safe? We can't lock her up in the house forever. That would kill her." Nigel paced, not seeing Jackson nodding his agreement.

"Give us a day to finalize our plans. We want to draw Josh out and then the mayor." Nixon's eyes were on Nevin as he spoke.

Nigel spun. "There is no way I'm putting Havan out there to draw him in. Absolutely no way."

"We don't plan to, son. We have a plan that we're working on with the police. They just need to obtain a warrant and then we can move ahead. They expect to have that early tomorrow morning." Nixon glanced at the clock. "It's almost suppertime. How be I grill some chicken or something for us? You do have some, don't you?"

Nigel stared at his father for a moment, before snapping his mouth shut. He knew exactly what his father was up to and while he agreed with his motive, wasn't sure about his method. "I do. In the fridge. I pulled some out earlier today."

Chapter 17

Pacing the living room the next morning, Havan thought through what she knew of Josh Bridgman and realized they didn't know that much about him. He had had enough to live on, but had never said what he did for a living. That puzzled her now. Why had they never asked?

She was alone in the house, except for Naomi, who was in the office on the phone with Noelle. Nigel had an appointment he couldn't miss but had been reluctant to leave her. She had just laughed, telling him to go, the house had a security system, and she would make sure not to go outside the locked doors.

She stood for a moment, eyes on the kitchen, knowing she really didn't need to do anything there, but finally walking into the room and slowing spinning, taking in the home Nigel had created. She liked it. She wasn't sure if it was all his doing or not, but whoever had helped him, she would need to thank

"He did the decorating himself, Havan." Naomi smiled at her from the doorway. "He's always had the knack of making a place comfortable and livable without a lot of knickknacks or doodads as he calls them."

"This house is so comfortable." Havan watched as Naomi approached, heading for the coffeemaker. "Thank you, Naomi. You and Nixon have raised a fine family."

Naomi paused, turned to look at the younger woman, surprise on her face. "Well, thank you, dear. I don't think anyone has ever said that to us before."

Havan just smiled before reaching to hug Naomi. She frowned as she heard the doorbell. "I wasn't expecting anyone. Were you?"

Naomi shook her head and then peeked towards the door. "I don't know him. Do you?"

Havan sidled closer to the door and then almost ran back to Naomi. "It's Josh. How did he know where I am? We can't let him in."

"No, we can't. He knows you're here, Havan." Naomi reached for her phone, called

Nixon. "Josh is here at Nigel's, Nixon. He's outside but I can tell he's very angry."

There was the sound of breaking glass and Naomi grabbed Havan's hand and ran for the basement, searching for the door she knew was there, not able to find it before Josh was there, a weapon pointed at them.

"Havan, my dear. It's about time I found you. I've tried to find out how you are. No one would tell me."

"Go away, Josh. Run. I won't tell anyone you've been here. You can get away, if you really want to." Havan stood in front of Naomi, trying to protect the mother of the man she loved.

"Not happening, Havan. You've cost me too much money. Millions, in fact. Brown was to pay me with what he inherited when his daughters married. You stopped that." Josh's look of anger and hatred was directed solely at her.

"And I'd do it again, just to protect my husband." She stared at him, her eyes narrowed, her thoughts racing as to how she could get him out of the house and keep Naomi safe. She sighed as she saw the two men appear behind Josh. "Brought reinforcements, Josh? Couldn't face me on your own?"

"That's not the reason, Havan." He nodded towards Naomi. "Tie her up." His large hand reached for Havan and pulled her away from Naomi as she kicked and struggled to release herself from his grip.

Naomi struggled to prevent the men from binding her to a chair but they prevailed. She watched in horror as Havan was pulled up the stairs, still trying her best to get away. She caught the look of fear on the younger woman's face and began to pray for her as she had never prayed before.

Naomi heard the running footsteps overhead and the shouts for Havan and herself, calling out that she was in the basement. Nixon was at her side as soon as he heard her voice, untying her and making sure she was okay.

Nigel appeared. "Mom? You're okay?"

"I am, son. He took Havan. He's mad, Nixon. I think he's going to kill her." She shoved away from him and ran for the stairs, searching the house. "He did take her away, didn't he?"

"Who, love?" Nixon finally stopped her frantic movements. "Who took Havan?"

"She called him Josh. He said she had cost him millions."

Nigel's eyes met his father's and he knew. Havan may well already be dead. He dropped to the floor, back to the wall, his head cradled on his arms as he heard movement around him. How long he sat there, he had no idea. He finally felt a hand on his arm, pulling him to his feet.

"Come on, Nigel. We have a lead. Let's go." Nevin stood there, Nolan beside him balancing on his crutches.

"Where? Did you find her?" Nigel's eyes were blurry. He couldn't think past the fact that Havan was gone once more.

"We have a lead. Let's go." Nevin's hand on Nigel's arm tugged him with him to his vehicle. "In you go. We're heading back to Sanctuary."

"Sanctuary? He's heading that way?"

Nevin nodded. "He was seen there about an hour ago. And no, Havan wasn't seen with him. He could have stashed her somewhere."

"He's using her to get to the mayor. The mayor is mad enough he'll kill her himself. He wanted those millions that were to come to him, and she thwarted him without even realizing that she had." Nigel stared out the window. "We're flying?"

"Angus has the copter ready to go. It's the quickest way." Nevin pulled into the airport and to their hangar. "Hold on for a moment, Nigel. We need to pray." He reached for his brother's arm to keep him in his seat, sharing a look with Nolan.

Hours later, Nigel slumped against the truck they had borrowed, his eyes on the ground, hands shoved deep into his pockets. He shivered, feeling the fine misty rain and knowing he should climb into the truck, but having no heart to do just that. He finally looked up as he heard Nolan's crutches hitting the ground beside him.

"Into the truck, Nigel. We're heading back to Jackson's."

Nigel shook his head. "No. I want to wait here."

Nixon appeared, Jackson beside him. "Into the truck, son. They're still searching. We need you to be warm and safe for when we bring her home."

"She's coming home? Alive? You know that for sure, Dad?"

"We'll believe that God will bring her home safely. Come, son. Jackson has a room ready for you."

Nigel finally shoved away from the truck and waited for Nolan to slide in before he did himself, his eyes on the woods he knew was being searched. They had refused to let him go into them. They wanted him with his father and Jackson. He knew why. The mayor was apt to come after him too.

Nigel finally settled down on the bed he had used in Havan's room, his eyes open as he stared at the wall, not willing to sleep, but not willing to be around anyone else right then. He felt himself beginning to grieve, not knowing if his bride was still alive. This was worse than when she and Nolan were taken, he thought. At least then she was not on her own. He tossed and turned, twisting the blanket he had covered himself with around himself. Finally, towards dawn, his body won and he slept, exhausted. He didn't hear his father enter the room to rouse him, stand for a moment watching, and then just as silently leave the room, shaking his head at Nolan.

"He's asleep, Nolan. For now, let him sleep. He won't rest until Havan's home. You know that. It's how you would be if that was Amy out there."

Nolan nodded, then headed for his brother. "I'll sit with him, Dad. I'll just sit and pray. I can't stand the thought of how he's suffering."

Nixon nodded, as he watched his youngest son move way, before he turned to Jackson, accepting with thanks the cup of coffee he was offered, shaking his head at the offer of food.

"Jackson? How are you still on your feet?" Nixon slid into a chair, a sigh drawn from him.

Jackson just shook his head, reaching for his own mug of tea before he too sat. "Once you've lost someone you love deeply, Nix, it can go either way. You grow stronger. You lose and wither up inside. When I lost Havan's mother, that's what almost happened to me. Havan kept me going. It's the hope that God gives me, that even if the worse comes true, I will see my girls again. I know that for a certainty. Now, today? I have no idea who I'm still functioning. That's how God works."

Nixon nodded, knowing his friend had been through things he hadn't. "I hear what you're saying, Jax. I just pray that doesn't happen to Nigel or to you again."

"I pray the same thing, but it is as God wills, Nix. We have to pray that way." Jackson's voice died away as he stared down at his mug, his thoughts on his daughter. It had been a long day and a longer night, not knowing where she was, knowing it had cooled off greatly and that the misty rain had turned to a downpour. Lord, he prayed, protect her. Give her shelter if she's out in this rain. Bring her home, Lord, whichever way You choose to. Give us the peace and strength that we'll need.

Nixon rose and began to pace, unable to articulate his prayer, but knowing God heard him. He stopped for a moment in the bedroom door, his eyes on his middle son and then his youngest son. He drew a deep breath before he moved on, pulling out his phone to call Naomi once more, needing to hear her voice and her prayers.

He pocketed his phone shortly, turning to head back to his cup of tea as he heard running footsteps and the door flew open. Angus charged through, unable to speak for a moment, searching for Nigel.

"Angus? You have word?" Jackson was at Nixon's side.

Angus nodded. "Where's Nigel?"

"Right here." Nigel was at the bedroom door. "Angus?"

"They know where she is, Nigel. Somehow, one of the dogs caught a scent and is leading them to her. We've been asked to meet at the copter. They want you back home. They'll bring her there."

"No, take me there, where she is."

"I can't , Nigel. They won't let me. They want you at home. They'll bring her to you. To both you and Jackson." Angus appealed to Jackson with a look.

"Do what they ask, Nigel. We'll go and wait with your parents. Come on, son. We'll have to drive, I think, unless they can get the copter up."

"The rain has lessened enough it's giving us a window if we go now."

Chapter 18

Struggling against the hand tight on her arm, Havan tried to free herself and run. Josh had too tight a grip on her for that to happen. She kicked at him, earning herself a blow to the side of her head, stunning her for a moment, long enough for one of the men to bind her hands in front of her and shove her into an unknown SUV. It had to be Josh's, she realized, but she had never seen it before. She reached for the handle on the other door, hoping to free herself that way, but was pulled back and a seatbelt fastened around her.

She spun as best she could to protest, stopping as she saw the weapon pointed at her. Josh watched impassively from the front seat before he turned and spoke quietly to the driver. Havan twisted to stare at the house as it faded into the distance, willing the tears back down, praying that she'd be back, to be held tight in Nigel's arms once more, to feel safe and secure.

She turned to face forward again, her eyes narrowed as she watched the road, wondering where Josh was heading. Not towards Sanctuary, she thought, but wait? Wasn't that the other way home? She slumped back, defeated for the moment, her thoughts turning to unspoken prayer.

Josh turned his head to watch her, waiting for her to speak, knowing she would at some point. He frowned when she just stared past him, not speaking, not acknowledging him at all. He grew angrier. She had cost him millions already. She would cost him no more.

Havan watched closely as the SUV entered Sanctuary, heading for a building on the other side of town from where they had entered the town. The vehicle was pulled into a commercial garage and then stopped. Josh stepped from the vehicle, leaving Havan under guard.

An hour later, Josh returned and the vehicle pulled away, Havan watching Josh closely, seeing the hints of satisfaction in him that he was trying to hide. This is it, isn't it, Lord? He's found Brown who will take me somewhere and then it will all be over. Make sure Nigel doesn't grieve for too long, please, dear Lord. Let him know, please, how much I do love him and how I wished we could really grow old together, just like he asked me to.

She was finally pulled from the vehicle after it stopped near the entrance to the trail over the hills behind her home. She searched the area with her eyes, not seeing anyone who would help. The two men of Josh's flanked her, waiting for word from him to move forward. She sighed to herself, reaching her bound hands up to rub at her face.

Josh watched from a distance away, shaking his head. It should never have come to this, Havan. If you had stayed away that day, Nigel would have been married to someone else, I would have been given my money, and everyone would have been happy and safe. But you had to get involved, didn't you? Why? That's what I don't get. He turned as he heard a vehicle approaching and saw Brown step from it.

Good, Josh thought. He's on his own. This will be over quickly. He walked towards the mayor, Havan watching in fear as he did so, knowing this was it for her, whatever it was. Her thoughts turned to prayer and she closed her eyes, not willing to watch the two men. The men holding her frowned and shared a look before shrugging. It was not the first time they had been in this situation. Josh was known to get rid of problems in a certain way, and they thought this would be the same as before.

Josh and Brown spoke for a while, the two men with Havan finally losing interest in them and her, moving away from her to stand closer to the vehicle. She searched around, knowing the area, and praying she could escape, somehow break free of her bonds and flee. She inched herself backwards from the men, one careful step at a time, before she found herself near the entrance of an animal path. She watched closely, seeing an argument breaking out between the two older men and the two younger men's attention drawn to that before they moved closer. She ducked down beneath the branches, listening carefully as she did so.

She moved as silently as she could away from the men, knowing she was not likely to get far before they discovered her missing. She jumped as she heard loud pops and then silence. She stopped, peering through the underbrush and not seeing anything. She thought she heard her name being called before she moved on, trying to find a way home, and not seeing one. She heard the crashing in the brush around her and then the loud shouts of her name.

She paused, crouching down, hiding her face even though she didn't think she could be seen. She worked at the knots with her teeth, finally loosening the rope enough she could slip it off. She stuck it a pocket of her jeans, not knowing if she would need it. She heard the voice again and froze. Brown! What had happened to Josh and his men? What had Brown done to them? And what would he do to her if he found her? She knew without a shadow of a doubt she would not survive if he found her.

Brown spun in a circle where he stood, searching for her. She had been there, he had seen her when he stepped from his car. Josh had been stupid, he thought, leaving his men so far away from him. He had dealt with all three of them. None of them would bother him again. He just needed to find Havan and deal with her. She had cost him plenty and the anger and downright rage in him towards her fuelled his life right now. Until she was dead, he would not be satisfied. Then he needed to find his wife and daughters. They too would pay for leaving him.

He traced his steps back, still not seeing where Havan had gone to. He frowned. She had disappeared into thin air, and that was not acceptable. Josh should have known better than to bring her here, to her home area, to somewhere she knew how to escape to. He finally stormed back to his car and left, dust kicking up behind him.

Havan heard the car leaving and moved on, knowing she would soon be near Josh's place and then home. Would anyone be there yet? Had anyone been there? She swiped at the tears on her face. She didn't cry, but she was. That was something different for her. She had thought being strong meant no tears, but maybe she had been wrong. Lord, please guide me home, back to Nigel, back to Dad.

Momentarily distracted, she felt her foot slip and with a sharp cry, she slid off the side of the hill and tumbled down the slope, to lie against the uprooted tree roots before she sat up, shakily, and stared back up at the path. There was no way she could get back up there. That left climbing over the tree and moving that way through the dense underbrush. She looked up at the sky as she felt the first drop of rain and sighed. Just what she needed. Rain. But if she could get past this tree, the overhead canopy would shelter her somewhat.

She trudged on, still not sure exactly where she was, not able to get a bearing from the sun to know which direction she was going. She knew eventually she would reach the edge of the trees but she was just so tired. She sank down on a path she didn't even know she was on and rested back against a tree, her head leaning on the trunk, her eyes sliding closed. She just could not move any further. Her feet were so sore. Her sneakers had not been meant to walk this type of terrain. Without water, she was in danger, she knew, but she just had to rest. Her eyes slid closed and she slept, not feeling the misty rain getting heavier and soaking her.

She roused later, soaked, tired, hungry, dirty, and pulled herself to her feet, stumbling as she did so, rubbing her arms with her hands to try and warm up, knowing it was a useless effort. It had grown dark and she needed to find some shelter for the night. But where? She jumped as she heard movement beside her and looking down, saw a young dog beside her. She held out her hand, and the dog sniffed at her and then licked her fingers before moving ahead of her, looking back at her. She nodded wearily, putting one foot in front of the other to follow the dog, feeling it was useless, really. Lord, I'm not going to make it home. Please comfort Nigel.

She finally dropped to her knees and then looked around, finding a relatively dry area under a large tree and crawling to it, sitting with her back to the tree, her head on her knees. She felt the dog curl up tight to her and she reached an arm to hug her.

Chapter 19

Nigel paced his home, waiting for word, not willing to eat when his mother or a sister pressed him to. He took the mugs of tea he was handed but refused everything else. Jackson watched, knowing that Nigel was hurting in a way he shouldn't be.

Jackson stood in Nigel's office later that morning, his hand on the window sill, as he heard footsteps approaching. He braced for word, word that his beloved daughter was indeed dead.

"Jax?" Nixon's voice had him turning.

Jackson nodded, his eyes on the other man's face, seeing something there he didn't like. "Nix? Have you found her?"

Nixon shook his head. "No, we haven't, but she did somehow get away from Josh. She's out in the woods somewhere behind your place. We have teams going in to search even as we speak. With the rain, they'll try the dogs, but they can't promise they'll be successful with them."

Jackson nodded as he approached the desk, eyeing the map laying on it. He had brought the map with him. He traced trails with shaking fingers. "There's something more, isn't there?"

"There is. They found Josh and two of his men, shot. They think it was Brown. Brown was the last one Josh seems to have contacted. His phone was still open and unlocked when they found it, on a last call to Brown."

"Dead? Oh no! Does that mean Brown has her?"

Nixon shook his head. "Not at all. Officers running a road block four hours from here stopped Brown and when they ran his plate, realized he was wanted here. They've arrested him."

Jackson sank back against the desk. "She's safe from him? We all are?"

Nigel spoke from the doorway before he walked towards the older men. "We are, Jackson. You finally are. Your town can heal now."

"But where is my daughter? Your wife?" Jackson spun, heading for the doorway, before Nixon stopped him by stepping in his way.

"Jackson. Wait. We don't need you out there searching. What we need is your expertise, to tell our teams where to search."

Jackson tried to move past Nixon but was again stopped. He searched the man's face and eyes before he nodded. "I'll stay until late this afternoon. Then I'm heading back home."

"I'll be with you, Jackson. Just look over the map. I'll show you where they found Josh and then you can let us know where to search from there." Nigel moved his father-in-law to the desk and the map.

Nixon had his phone out and on speaker, calling Nolan, who was helping to coordinate the search efforts. Jackson rapidly gave details and trails to follow. His finger slowed finally. Nigel had left the room in answer to a question from Nora and hadn't returned as yet.

"Nixon, where's Nevin?"

"He's still near where they found the bodies. Why?"

"Get him on the phone. There's a small animal path that crosses that trail. Tell him to look for any sign that she was near it. If she was, and the men distracted, she could have slipped into it and away. It's worth a try. If Nevin will walk it, with one of the others, without pulling the group away from their searches, I would appreciate it. It leads back of our home and then towards the hills more. It's not that safe a route, though."

Nevin listened intently as Jackson spoke to him, his eyes searching the area for the trail, Brett and Angus searching as well. A quiet word from Brett had Nevin and Angus turning to him and watching as he pulled back some brush.

"We've found it, Jackson. I'll check in every thirty minutes or so. We'll find her for you."

Nevin headed out first, the other two men behind him, their eyes on the ground as they walked, occasionally looking up. An hour later, Nevin held up a hand and pointed.

"There. That's a sneaker print. What size does she wear?"

"She has a small foot. Noelle mentioned it. It looks about that size." Angus looked around. "She's come this way, hasn't she? How far ahead is she?"

"Given that she ran yesterday at some point, who knows. If she had made it home, we would have known. Charlie's positioned himself there and won't leave, no matter what we asked him to do. He keeps saying she's coming back there and he wants to be the one to be there for her."

"She's made a friend of him. That's difficult for anyone outside of our group to do." Nevin paused to swig some water before sticking his bottle back into his pack. "Let's keep moving."

Thirty minutes later, they stopped, seeing the paw prints. "Dog or coyote?"

"Dog, I think. He's tracking her. Let's pray she stays safe from him if he's wild."

Four hours later they paused once more, hearing a low whining.

"Where's it coming from?" Angus spun in a circle, trying to find the source.

"Up ahead, I think?" Nevin moved forward, stopping as he found a young dog in his way. "Well, hello, there, girl. What are you doing out here all by yourself?"

The dog whined again, spun in a circle, and then headed down the trail, stopping and running back and forth, asking them to follow her. The three men exchanged a glance and then almost ran after her, sliding to a stop when she suddenly charged off the trail.

Nevin held up a hand. "What's with this? Stay here, fellows. No sense the three of us walking into danger, if that's what it is." He watched at the dog returned, tail wagging, giving a little woof.

He followed, his eyes watchful, steps careful, before he stopped, a sound rising from him before he dropped to his knees, a hand reaching for Havan. How had she made it this far? She was soaked, he could tell, and not awake.

"Angus? Brett? Here. The dog led me to her. We need to get her out of here."

Nevin reached to pick up Havan, the dog watching carefully before leading him back to the other two men. Angus had pulled out a thermal blanket and had it down on the ground.

"How is she?" Brett reached to help Nevin.

"Soaked. If she doesn't develop pneumonia, I'd be surprised." Nevin knelt as he watched Brett assess her. Brett was the one with the medical training, having gone through as a paramedic, knowing they needed someone with medical training on their team.

"Brett?" Angus looked up from where he had been feeding a sandwich to the dog, who had daintily taken the food.

"She's rousing, Angus. Let's get her wrapped in the blanket and sitting up. Other than exposure and the scrapes on her wrists, I don't see much injury wise."

Nevin braced his arm for Havan to lean on as she roused, her hands trying to escape from the blanket as she fought them, finally hearing her name called by a familiar voice.

"Nevin? You're here?" She blinked against the light, seeing the other two men. "Where am I?"

"On some forsaken animal path your father sent us on. Your new friend led us to you."

"Friend? I don't have any friends out here." She looked at the dog, who had moved to lay with her chin on Havan's leg. "Oh, this friend. She helped me, you know. She laid with me to try and keep me warm last night." She twisted to look up at Nevin. "Nigel?"

"He's fine. And so is Mom, other than being angry she couldn't stop Josh from taking you."

"She wasn't hurt? Oh, that's good. Please, can we leave? I want to talk to Nigel and then Dad."

"We'll leave in a bit, but here. I can put a call through for you. Reception's good in this area."

Nigel reached for his phone, seeing Nevin's number.

"Hello?" He waited, not hearing a sound. "Nevin, are you there?"

He heard a rustle, then a beloved voice.

"Nigel? Is that you?"

"Havan!" He shouted her name, bringing everyone running. "Havan! Oh, my love! Are you okay? Where are you?"

"I think I'm okay. Come get me, Nigel. Please? Come get me. Take me home. Please?" Her voice faded even as Nigel was talking to her.

"Nigel?"

"Nevin? What's going on? Please, tell me. Do you have her?" Nigel was almost pleading, not feeling the tears on his face or his mother's arm around him.

"We have her, Nigel. We'll bring her home to you. Give us a few hours, though. We're out in the middle of nowhere."

"She's okay, Nevin? Please tell me?"

"She's cold and wet. Tired. And she's bringing home a new friend." Nevin's voice faded for a moment as Nigel heard him reassuring Havan they would bring her friend with them.

Jackson reached for the phone. "Nevin, tell me exactly where you are." He listened and then spoke. "Walk about ten minutes forward. You'll find another trail to your right. Take it. That will bring you out to the house. Maybe twenty minutes?"

"She was that close, Jackson? That close to home?"

"She was, Nevin. She knows those woods better than I do. Her instincts would have had her heading home."

Nigel took the phone back, asking more questions before he turned to his mother, accepting her hug. Nixon stood for a moment before wrapping them both in his arm, a prayer of thanksgiving rising from him.

The girls scurried around, some to make a meal, some to make sure the bedroom was ready and warm for Havan, that clean clothes were ready for her in the bathroom. Nora grabbed towels, running for the dryer with them and throwing them in, ready to turn it on and heat them for her.

Nigel stood, dumbfounded that it had worked out so well. Jackson finally approached him, a hand to his arm leading him back to the office where he shoved Nigel down into a chair and then sat on an ottoman in front of him, his eyes assessing the younger man.

"Nigel?" When Nigel finally looked up, he saw the heartbreak and peace on Jackson's face. "I'm glad she's coming home to you. We'll be here for a while. Then we'll get out of your hair. Just know that Havan does love you more than anyone else in the world. She doesn't have to say that to me. I can see it. When you two are ready to redo your ceremony, it will be my honour to walk her to meet you." He stood, his hand on Nigel's head in a blessing before he walked away, shoulders slumped, fatigue weighing at him.

Nigel watched him go, knowing what he had just done, given his blessing to a young man he barely knew, entrusting his only and beloved daughter into his care. Lord, I have no idea what the future holds, but You do. Lead us please.

He paced the living room to the front door and back, not hearing Nolan's comment that he was going to wear a path into the floor and seeing as he had helped him to refinish it, he wished he wouldn't. Noelle had told him off, even as the other three younger women had laughed at him.

Finally, he heard the vehicle and was out of the door, hardly waiting for Nevin to stop before he had the back door open, and was reaching for Havan. Havan slept, worn out, but rousing as she was carried to the house, fighting for a moment until she looked up and saw Nigel.

"Nigel? You're safe? He threatened all of you." She turned her face into his shoulder as he found a chair and just sat, his arms tight around her.

"He won't hurt you or anyone else any more."

She nodded. "He's dead, isn't he? So are the two men who were with him. Brown?"

"He's in custody. Another force arrested him. He'll not be out for many years. The judge has set his bail extremely high." Nigel shared a look with Jackson, who nodded. He would not have chosen to tell

Havan in such a way, but Nigel was her husband and it was his decision.

Nigel finally gathered Havan up into his arms and headed up to their room, setting her on her feet and peeling back the thermal blanket.

"Nora has brought up some warm towels for you. Someone left clean clothes for you in the bathroom. Go on, my love. Shower, have a bath. Get cleaned up and then we'll see if you want something other than tea." He watched her face before he gathered her close. "I thought I had lost you, my love. I didn't want to live."

She hugged him back before standing on her toes to kiss him. "Me, too, love. Let me get cleaned up and then I'll see. Send everyone home, please? I just need some quiet."

Chapter 20

Pacing the next day, Havan was unable to settle down in a chair, to settle down to any task. She felt unsettled, not sure as to why, but knowing their adventure as Nolan had named it was not over, not yet. Something told her that, and she had learned to depend on her instincts. She was alone in the house for the moment and didn't like that feeling. She used to enjoy being on her own. Something just felt off that day.

Nigel had taken the dog she had brought home with her to a vet that morning, saying they would look for her family, but would keep her if she was indeed a stray. Feeling selfish, Havan had prayed just that, but had repented, knowing Angel as she called her likely belonged to a loving family.

She turned to the door as she heard a knock, frowning. She wasn't expecting anyone, unless it was one of Nigel's family. Expecting to see one of them, she pulled the door open, stopping in surprise.

"Grace Brown? What are you doing here? How did you find me?"

"Can I come in, please, Havan? I need to talk to you." Grace Brown was around Havan's age, and Havan knew she was the one her father had wanted to marry Nigel.

"Yeah, I guess. Here. Let me take your jacket. Can I get you anything to drink?"

Grace shook her head, looking around the living room. "This is nice. Who decorated? You?"

Havan frowned. "No. Nigel did. It was like this when I came."

"He has good taste." Grace wandered around the room. "You got lucky, Havan."

"Not luck, Grace. God." She watched closer, seeing something she felt uncomfortable with. "What do you want, Grace? And how did you find me?"

"Everyone here in town knows the Wells. It was just a matter of watching one of them to find them driving to Nigel's house. I knew you'd be here." She turned, a cool assessing look on her face. "How did you know that day, Havan? No one knew."

"Once again, God, Grace. He had me there." Havan moved away from Grace, something telling her to move. "What do you want, Grace?"

"My husband. That's what. Nigel should have been mine. I would have had freedom then. I would have been able to get away from both my parents."

Havan shook her head. "Not happening, Grace. Even if I did, he would never marry you. That much I know. He's too good a man, a dedicated Christian man. You're not the person he would need." She froze as Grace raised a weapon, pointing it at her head. "Don't do this, Grace. Turn around and walk away from me. I'll never tell anyone."

"Too late for that, Havan. And who calls anyone that ridiculous name, anyway! Mom was just as bad as Dad. She treated us just like he did. She thought she had you fooled when you were both with Josh. She was playing a game, cooperating with him, to get you and Nigel into his clutches. That didn't work for long, and she came after me. I don't care what you say. Nigel is mine!"

"No, he's not. He never will be." Havan was moving around the room, heading for the door, praying she could make it out. She thought she had heard another vehicle, praying that it was Nigel, or one of his family.

The door swung open and Janet stood there, her eyes on her daughter. "Grace?

What's the meaning of this? I thought I told you to stay away."

"I don't have to do what you say." Grace swung the weapon to point it at her mother. "This is your fault too. Yours and Dad's."

"Whatever are you talking about? I had nothing to do with his plans."

"That's not what he says. I talked to him three days ago. He said you were in on it too."

"No, I wasn't. I tried to protect you girls, took the brunt of whatever it was he dished out." The weapon wavered slightly in Grace's hand.

Janet suddenly caught Havan by the arm, shoving her out the open door and slamming and locking it behind her. Havan tumbled to the porch floor, her hands and knees taking the brunt of the fall before she spun and stared at the door, hearing the angry and loud words coming from behind it.

She felt hands raising her up and rushing her away from the house. She was thrust into Nigel's arms, which tightened around her as they were moved to a vehicle. A dog's tongue came out to lick her face, and she ducked.

"Nigel? What's going on? How did you know?" She reached to touch his face, seeing the concern for her written there.

"Janet called. One of the younger girls told her Grace was coming to see you and meant to kill you." Nigel's arms tightened around her. "I was so afraid we'd be too late. The ETF team is waiting to move in. Did she lock the door?"

"Janet did when she shoved me out the door." She jumped as she heard the sound of a weapon discharging. "Nigel?" Fear stood out on her face.

"Ssh, love. Let the police deal with it."

Fifteen minutes later, Nixon appeared at the open car door, crouching down so he could see them, a closed look on his face.

"Dad?" Nigel's voice brought Nixon's eyes to his son's face before he looked at Havan.

"We'll have to find you a new home, Havan. You won't want to go back in there." He sighed. "And neither will Nigel. Any memories there will always be tainted now."

"Dad? What happened?"

"Grace shot her mother, then turned the weapon on herself. She just couldn't live with what she had been through anymore. Janet's on her way to the hospital. She survived. Her other three girls will need her."

"And Grace? How could he have done this, driven her to this?" Havan's thoughts were with the other woman.

"Greed, plain and simple, Havan. He wanted it all and didn't care who he hurt in the hunt for it. It's unfortunate it was his family." Nixon stood and walked away, needing to compose himself.

Havan cuddled closer to Nigel. "Take me home, Nigel. Can you get away from work and take me home?"

"I can do that, my love, but better than going to the cabin, I'll take you to the cottage. I bought it from Dad a week ago. I was waiting for the right time to tell you it is ours."

"Oh, that's nice. What about Angel?"

"She goes with us. No one seems to want her. The vet will look for a while but he didn't think anyone wanted her, she's been out in the woods for most of her life, he thought."

"Oh, lovely. Come here, Angel girl. Let's go home."

Nigel slid from the vehicle to have a word with his father before heading for Havan and Angel and leading them to his own vehicle. He stood for a moment, his hand on the closed vehicle door, his eyes on his house. He would not come back. His father had promised to have a team come in and clean it and another one to pack everything for him. He also promised that the family would bring them clothes and whatever else they needed for now. His main concern would be Havan and her health.

Nigel stood on the deck at the cottage, listening to the evening sounds around him and the gentle lapping of the waves against the shore and the dock. It had been two months since Grace had appeared at his home, a tough two months when Havan and he had had to relive what had happened. But it was not all bad, he thought.

A month ago, Havan had appeared in the doorway of his parents' living room, her hand on her father's arm, her mother's wedding dress and veil in place, his peach roses in her other hand, her eyes only on him. They had celebrated their marriage in the proper way, in front of just their family. That was how they wanted it. Havan said they had been in the spotlight enough for a lifetime and she didn't want that on their special day.

He stared down at the lone wooden chair sitting on the dock and smiled. He had tried to move two down there but Havan had refused, pulling him to the lonely chair, shoving him down and then cuddling with him. She informed him that if they sat in two chairs, they couldn't do just that. He had laughed long at that, then kissed her thoroughly, finally agreeing with her logic, laughing again at the smirk on her face.

He looked up as he heard her feet on the dock, watching closely as she walked towards him, mugs of tea in her hand. She has blossomed, he thought, becoming more beautiful in every way. She was looking at taking college courses on line, but wasn't quite sure what she wanted to study. She had informed him Sanctuary needed to be rebuilt from the ground up and that it really needed a library. Did he know a librarian? He had informed her no, but that she could become one. They would work with the town until she graduated if that's what she chose.

He himself was still at loose ends, working remotely for his father's company, but eyeing a building in town to open up something, what he was still working through. Havan supported him fully in his decisions, but what did he really want to do, she asked?

He reached for the tea, kissing her, before he pointed to the end of the dock, holding her had as she sat, feet touching the water, before he sat beside her, content.

"I heard from Janet Brown today." Havan was sad. "She said Brown died last night in a jail riot. He had tried to become the big man there and someone took him out, as she said. She also said she and the three girls are moving far away from here, going into counselling and seeing if they can heal. I advised her to find a good church with a pastor who can help counsel them God's way, not the world's way. She agreed, saying that was what they all wanted. Our conversations about God and all this Bible are paying off."

"I'm glad she's taking that step. They need a new start. Thank you for being open to speaking with her."

"I feel sorry for her. She's lived what they call hell on earth with him, lost a husband and her oldest to that life, and now needs the healing only God can bring. She needs to find their sanctuary, one only He can provide."

"That's what I would like to do. Help people find their sanctuary, somehow. I've decided to look into opening that building as a drop-in centre, resource office, whatever we need to do to help people heal and find where they need to be. The minister of the town has approached me. He would like to offer classes there as well, Bible study. His wife is a trained counsellor, believe it or not, just finishing her courses. They had planned to move away, not liking how the mayor controlled them. Now, they want to stay and help the city heal."

"That's wonderful, Nigel. With your college degree, it would work. You could help train in a business way, setting them up for success. Sanctuary needs to remarket itself to the area, growing beyond the stigma it's been under. I think you're the one who can do that."

"Only with you beside me, my love. That's the only way." He paused, not quite sure how to continue. "The whole town has approached your Dad, asking him to become the mayor. He's not sure on that. I think he should."

"He talked to me earlier. I asked if he had prayed about it and what did God tell him to do. He just laughed at me, hugged me, kissed my cheek, and said that's exactly what he had been told to do. So, he's the new mayor." She grinned up at him, a spark of mischief in her eyes. "Think you can work with him?"

Nigel laughed as he set their mugs aside and pulled her close to him, kissing her long and hard, finally leaning back to look down at her. "We never knew all those weeks ago, did we, my love, just where God would lead us?   He was there that day, Havan, bringing you into my life, to complete my heart. I never knew you were the one I was waiting for."

She leaned agains him, her eyes on the rising moon, content. "I knew I wanted someone strong, someone who would lead our family first as a Christian, and then as a man. You are he, my love. God has indeed blessed us. Now, we need to use that to bless those around us. I think we're heading down the right path, but God will lead us where and when He wants and desires."

"That He will. We just need to remain open to that leading."

They were silent, content with each other, their thoughts on where God had lead them and from what. They had found the sanctuary with one another that God had meant for them.

Dear Readers

Thank you for choosing to read His Sanctuary, the story of Nigel and Havan and their struggle to find the sanctuary God had meant for them.

I have been fascinated with the concept of God's sanctuary cities in the Old Testament, how you could be safe there. Then I wondered what would happen if the sanctuary city was where you weren't safe at all? That danger lurked there, led by an evil and corrupt man? That's where the idea for this novel developed and took off, and it took off led by Nigel and Havan on a route that I never saw coming. I didn't plan for that many in Nigel's family, for Havan not to have had her mother all of her life, for what happened to happen. That's how the stories evolve - the characters drive the plot and the circumstances of how they learn to trust more fully in God.

Finding our own sanctuary in God is a life-long journey. We are never truly there until He calls us home, but we are safe in Him, no matter how battered we become on this journey called life. Just put your hand in His and let Him lead you. That's the only

way to make it through. It's a lesson I learn
over and over again.

May God bless each one of you as you
journey through life.

Ronna